A big sticky mess . . .

Mr. Seigel placed the egg in Jessica's hand. "Now," he said. "Little Steven Fido is your responsibility. One of you must have him with you at all times, or see to it that he is properly taken care of. I'll expect you to return him intact at the end of the experiment. If he breaks, you will lose five points off your grade."

"Sure you don't want me to hold him, Jessica?" Rick teased. "You know how clumsy you are. Look at the mess you made in the cafeteria yesterday."

"I made!" Jessica said. She felt herself gritting her teeth. What had happened in the cafeteria was all his fault. He knew it as well as she did. So why was he needling her? Her hand involuntarily balled into a fist and . . .

CRACKKKKK!

"Eeuuuuu," the audience moaned.

Jessica looked down in horror. Runny yellow egg yolk oozed from between her fingers and dripped down onto the stage. Rick let out a loud burst of laughter, and Mr. Seigel shook his head sadly.

"I-I'm sorry," Jessica stammered, wishing she could just drop right down through a big hole in the stage and never be seen again.

SWEET VALLEY TWINS titles, published by Bantam Books.
Ask your bookseller for titles you have missed:

SWEET VALLEY TWINS

The Middle School Gets Married

Written by
Jamie Suzanne

Created by
FRANCINE PASCAL

BANTAM BOOKS
TORONTO • NEW YORK • LONDON • SYDNEY • AUCKLAND

THE MIDDLE SCHOOL GETS MARRIED
A BANTAM BOOK 0 553 40632 9

Originally published in U.S.A. by Bantam Skylark Books

First publication in Great Britain

PRINTING HISTORY
Bantam edition published 1993

Sweet Valley High and Sweet Valley Twins are registered trademarks of Francine Pascal.

Conceived by Francine Pascal.

Produced by Daniel Weiss Associates, Inc., 33 West 17th Street, New York, NY 10011

Bantam Books are published by Transworld Publishers Ltd., 61–63 Uxbridge Road, Ealing, London W5 5SA, in Australia by Transworld Publishers (Australia) Pty. Ltd., 15–25 Helles Avenue, Moorebank, NSW 2170, and in New Zealand by Transworld Publishers (N.Z.) Ltd., 3 William Pickering Drive, Albany, Auckland.

Printed and bound in Great Britain by
Cox & Wyman Ltd., Reading, Berks.

THE MIDDLE SCHOOL GETS
MARRIED

The Middle School Gets Married

One

"It's so romantic," Jessica Wakefield exclaimed with a sigh.

Jessica's best friend, Lila Fowler, nodded. "Totally romantic," she agreed.

Mr. Seigel, their science teacher, overheard them. He frowned down at them from the stage of the Sweet Valley Middle School auditorium, where the entire school was gathered for a Monday-morning assembly. "It's not supposed to be romantic," he said sternly. "It's supposed to be a learning experience."

"But we're getting married," Randy Mason protested from the row behind Jessica. "That's kind of romantic, isn't it?"

Jessica turned and stared at Randy in

surprise. She would never have suspected him of being the romantic type. He was best known for his "Physics Is Your Friend" T-shirt, which he wore at least twice a week. But Randy was definitely looking starry-eyed. When Jessica looked around the auditorium, she noticed that a lot of other Sweet Valley Middle School students were, too.

"I thought this assembly was just going to be another boring physical-fitness and healthy-diet lecture," Lila whispered.

"Me, too," Jessica whispered back. "That's what these health-and-hygiene assemblies usually are."

But Mr. Seigel had surprised her and everybody else when he had announced that they were all about to participate in a marriage project. All the students were going to be paired up into married couples for two weeks.

"This is going to be fun," Jessica whispered confidently. "And I don't care what Mr. Seigel says; it *is* kind of romantic. Just look around."

Even Jessica's identical twin sister, Elizabeth, looked a little misty as she smiled at Todd Wilkins. When Todd smiled back, Elizabeth blushed and dropped her pencil on the floor.

Jessica had to stifle a giggle. That kind of behavior certainly wasn't typical of Elizabeth.

Jessica and Elizabeth Wakefield were twelve years old and in the sixth grade at Sweet Valley

Middle School. But even though both girls had the same long, shiny blond hair, the same blue-green eyes, and the same dimple in their left cheeks, in practically every other way they were as different as night and day.

Jessica was a member of the Unicorns, a club made up of the prettiest and most popular girls at school. The Unicorns loved talking about makeup, rock stars, clothes, and parties. And their favorite subject of all was boys.

Elizabeth was more down-to-earth. She had lots of friends who were boys, including one she especially liked—Todd Wilkins. But that didn't mean she wanted to spend all her time talking about them. She had too many other things to do, like writing for *The Sweet Valley Sixers*, the official sixth-grade newspaper. She also loved reading mysteries and spending time with her close friends Amy Sutton, Sophia Rizzo, and Maria Slater.

But no matter how down-to-earth Elizabeth usually was, Jessica thought that right now she looked as silly and romantic as everybody else.

"I can't wait to get married," said Kimberly Haver, a seventh-grade Unicorn. "I think a wedding is the most romantic thing in the whole world."

"Mr. Seigel, will we get to have weddings?" Janet Howell, the eighth-grade president of the

Unicorn Club, called out eagerly, stealing a glance in Denny Jacobson's direction.

"No. You won't have weddings," Mr. Seigel said, looking impatient.

There were groans of disappointment, mostly coming from the row where the Unicorns sat.

Mr. Seigel held up ˙his hand for silence. "Marriage isn't just about weddings and flowers and romance. Marriage is about responsibility. That's what I hope you all will learn from this project."

"Will we at least get to pick who we're married to?" Sophia Rizzo asked.

"Couples will be selected at random," Mr. Seigel answered. "I will pick names out of a hat, and post the list of couples tomorrow morning."

"The lottery of loooooove," Aaron Dallas sang, quoting the lyrics to Johnny Buck's latest hit.

The rest of the students burst into laughter, and Mr. Seigel clapped his hands. "Quiet, please. Raise your hands if you have something to say." He spotted Randy Mason waving his hand in the air. "Randy?"

"I still don't get it," Randy said. "Is this supposed to be part of our science class or what?"

"That's a good question. This is what's called a multidisciplinary unit. It will be part math, part home economics, part social studies, and part science. There will be several sections of the project, and you will be expected to complete them all. For example, each couple will be required to work out a household budget, plan a menu, and cook a meal. You'll even get a taste of child-rearing. Over the next two weeks, we will have a series of lectures like this one. When necessary, the cafeteria will be turned into a study hall in order to accommodate this large group."

Mr. Seigel held up a manual. "At the next assembly, every couple will receive a manual like this one. In it, there are several collected essays and articles on marriage and family life. There is a lot of good information in here that I hope will help you complete the project successfully."

Jessica looked over at Lila and rolled her eyes. Mr. Seigel could make anything sound boring—even marriage.

The teacher looked out over the group of students. "I want to emphasize that this project is designed for couples. As of tomorrow morning, when each of you has learned who your spouse is, you must remember that you are part of a couple. You must learn to think as a couple. And you must learn to work as a couple. All seminars and study halls must be attended as a couple. No matter how you feel about your spouse, *all* sections of the project must be completed as a couple. Understood?"

He smiled, but then his face became serious. "I think you will discover that life will change dramatically after tomorrow morning," he said. "So be prepared."

Jessica looked around and saw that many of the students were suddenly looking just as serious as Mr. Seigel. There was something almost ominous about what he was saying. Jessica felt a little flicker of worry. *You're just being silly,* she told herself, flipping her hair over her shoulder. After all, Mr. Seigel was always getting worked up about unimportant stuff. In science class, he jumped around and acted like every experiment was the key to the most important scientific discovery in the whole world.

Jessica still thought that this marriage project sounded more like fun than work. Besides, stuff like this never got graded. So what could be so hard about it? They might have to write a short paper or something. But mostly it sounded like lectures and study groups.

Jessica smiled. She liked study groups. It meant you could usually count on somebody else doing most of the work. Unlike her twin sister, Jessica hated studying.

"We will assemble again tomorrow morning," Mr. Seigel said. "Until then, you are dismissed."

The auditorium erupted into excited chatter as the students stood and began to file out. Jessica picked up her notebook and purse and followed Lila down the row toward the aisle.

"I don't care what Mr. Seigel says," Lila said as they headed into the hallway. "This is going to be totally cool. I've always wanted to get married." She tossed her long brown hair over her shoulder. "I wonder if Daddy will let me have a little wedding. You know, two or three hundred of my closest friends, a gorgeous white dress, a cake with ten layers . . ."

"I can see it all now," said Mandy Miller, a fellow Unicorn, falling into step with them. "You and Lloyd Benson, standing at the altar."

Lila spun around and glared at Mandy. "Shut up. I am not getting stuck with Lloyd Benson."

Mandy smiled. "You never know."

"I'll probably get Bruce Patman or Jake Hamilton," Lila said confidently. She turned to Jessica. "Who would you like to be married to?"

Jessica's eyes flickered over the boys who were laughing and talking around them. It was exciting to think that by tomorrow morning, she would be married to one of them.

Exciting. But kind of strange. *I just hope*, she thought to herself, *that I don't end up with a total geek*.

"It's like the dark ages or something," Sophia said angrily, shoving her books and papers into her locker. "It's totally stupid! We don't even get to pick who we're married to. It's like the stuff my mom tells me and Tony about Italy in the old days."

"Come on, Sophia," Sarah Thomas said in her quiet, soft-spoken way. "It could be fun and kind of romantic, too." She smoothed the pink collar of her sweater. "I think this project could really teach us a lot."

"Hah!" Sophia snapped. That was exactly the sort of silly, romantic thing she'd expect Sarah to say.

As different as they were, Sophia and Sarah were practically best friends now, although they had been bitter enemies when they first met. When Sarah's dad and Sophia's mom had started dating each other, the girls had been horrified. They had cooked up plan after plan to put an end to their parents' romance, and somehow, in the process of working together, Sarah and Sophia had discovered that they liked each other.

Now that their parents had been dating for a few months, Sophia and Sarah were beginning to feel almost like sisters—even though they had about as much in common as Jessica and Elizabeth Wakefield.

Sophia prided herself on being independent and outspoken—and almost as tough as her older brother, Tony, who attended Sweet Valley High. She never hesitated to say what was on her mind, even if people didn't like it. As far as Sophia was concerned, she was just being honest.

Sarah, on the other hand, was shy and a little dreamy. She collected anything that had a rainbow on it, loved to draw, and hardly ever raised her voice.

Sophia closed her locker with an impatient slam. "I should have known you'd get all mushy over this marriage experiment," she said sourly.

"Well, marriage *is* romantic," Sarah said with a laugh. "When my mom was alive, she and my dad loved doing romantic things together—like picnics and bike rides and candlelight dinners."

"Well, before my dad left," Sophia said, "my parents were always arguing and shouting. There was nothing very romantic about that. I hated listening to them fight."

"Married couples don't *have* to fight," Sarah insisted gently. "Not if they really care about each other and make an effort to respect each others' feelings."

Sarah gazed earnestly at Sophia, and Sophia frowned. She'd never really thought about it that way. Maybe Sarah was right. Maybe couples didn't really have to fight. Now that she thought about it, she never heard her mother arguing with Mr. Thomas. They were always very considerate to each other.

But Sophia was a little worried about being married, even if it was only make-believe. She knew she had a hard time getting along with people sometimes. She could be bossy and too outspoken. She especially didn't get along with boys. But she couldn't help it. All the boys at Sweet Valley seemed kind of dumb to her.

Except for Patrick Morris, that is. He was the only boy at school she felt she could really get along with. And he was awfully good-looking, too. She couldn't help smiling as she thought about him. She knew she didn't really have much chance of being matched with Patrick, since the couples were being chosen randomly, but she found herself hoping that she'd be lucky and end up with him. If she did, this whole marriage project might not be so bad after all. In fact, she was sure that being married to Patrick would be a breeze.

Two

◇

The next morning, Jessica hurried through the front doors of Sweet Valley Middle School fifteen minutes before the first bell. She and Elizabeth had both dressed quickly and sped through breakfast. Neither of them had said so, but Jessica knew it was because they were both dying to find out who their spouses were.

Apparently, everyone else was, too. It seemed as if every student at Sweet Valley Middle School had arrived early. But as she looked around, Jessica realized she didn't see too many happy faces.

Suddenly she heard a loud moan behind her. She turned around and saw Ellen Riteman, a fellow Unicorn, leaning against her locker and looking depressed.

"What's the matter?" Jessica asked.

"It's so awful," Ellen said. "I'll never live it down. Janet Howell will never let me forget this. Guess who I'm married to?"

"Who?" Jessica breathed.

"Winston Egbert!" Ellen wailed.

All of the Unicorns thought that Winston was kind of a nerd. He was constantly telling really stupid jokes and goofing around. But he was also a really good gymnast and a member of the Boosters, the middle-school cheering squad.

"It could be worse," Jessica said comfortingly, but at the same time she couldn't help feeling a little relieved. If Winston was married to Ellen, it meant he couldn't be married to *her*. "Did you see who I'm married to?" Jessica asked, feeling a flutter of nervousness.

Ellen shook her head. "No. But the list is posted right outside Mr. Seigel's room."

"All right, time to meet Prince Charming," Jessica said, heading down the hall toward the science room.

Just as she was turning the corner, a hand shot out from between two banks of lockers.

"Yeow!" Jessica called out in surprise as the hand closed over her sleeve and yanked her between the lockers.

The hand belonged to Janet Howell. And

Janet looked furious. "Shhhhh!" she warned. She let go of Jessica's sleeve and looked cautiously around the corner of the lockers. Her face darkened and she turned back toward Jessica. "It's outrageous," she hissed. "Absolutely outrageous. Look out there."

Jessica stuck her head out from between the bank of lockers and peered down the hall. She immediately saw what had infuriated Janet. Denny Jacobson was standing in the hall with Cammi Adams, a shy sixth grader.

"They're married," Janet said through gritted teeth. "What a waste. How could Mr. Seigel have put a great guy like Denny with a total nerd like Cammi?"

Cammi Adams sometimes attended Jessica's ballet class. Jessica had never really talked to her, since Cammi always stood in the back and Jessica preferred the front row.

"Too bad Mr. Seigel didn't match up you and Denny," Jessica said. She knew that Janet had had a major crush on Denny Jacobson for a long time. They had even gone to a recent school dance together.

"I'll bet he's just miserable," Janet said. "Does he look miserable? Stick your head out again and tell me how miserable he looks."

Jessica stuck her head out and looked again. Actually, Denny didn't look miserable at all. He was talking to Cammi in a very friendly way.

That was probably why everybody liked Denny so much. He was nice and friendly to everyone.

But Jessica didn't have the nerve to say that to Janet. So she decided to change the subject. "Who did you get?"

Janet put her hand to her forehead and groaned. "Mr. 'Physics Is Your Friend' Randy Mason."

Jessica gasped. Well, at least Ellen didn't have to worry about any teasing from Janet now.

"Can you believe it? Doesn't Mr. Seigel have any taste at all? How could he do this to me?"

Jessica smoothed her rumpled sleeve. "He pulled the names out of a hat," she reminded Janet. "I'm sure it was nothing personal."

"I wonder if you'll feel that way when you find out who your husband is," Janet said with a sniff.

Jessica felt a heavy thump in her stomach. "Who is it?"

Janet shrugged her shoulders impatiently. "I don't know. After I checked my name and Denny's, I didn't have the heart to check anybody else's. I just hope you don't get stuck with somebody gross like I did."

"Me, too," Jessica said in a hoarse voice.

"Jessica!" she heard someone shout.

Jessica skidded to a stop and turned. Aaron Dallas was standing behind her, waving his arms to get her attention. "I've been looking all over for you."

"You have?" she asked happily.

What if Aaron was her husband? He was a lot of fun. And the two of them had liked each other on and off for a long time.

"I just wanted to tell you that I'm sorry we didn't wind up together."

Jessica's heart sank. "We didn't?"

"I'm married to Veronica Brooks," he explained, making a face.

"Veronica Brooks!" Jessica felt a little stab of jealousy. Veronica Brooks was Jessica's archenemy. She hated to think that Veronica and Aaron were a couple. Still, she didn't want to sound jealous. And she was pretty sure that Aaron disliked Veronica almost as much as she did.

Jessica pasted a smile on her face. "Well, that's too bad," she said.

Aaron shrugged awkwardly. "Yeah, well. I guess there are a lot of weird couples. Look over there."

Jessica's eyes followed the direction of his finger, and her eyes widened. Elizabeth was standing at the other end of the hall with Bruce Patman.

Wow! Jessica thought. Bruce Patman was in the seventh grade. He was really cute, and everybody thought he was the coolest guy in the middle school. Jessica had had a crush on him for a long time, but when she had finally gotten a chance to know him better, she had discovered that he was so conceited and arrogant that he never listened to one word anybody else said. Most of the Unicorns would have died to have Bruce as their husband, but Jessica knew that Elizabeth didn't like him at all.

On the other side of the hall, Jessica saw Todd Wilkins standing with Lila Fowler. Todd was really cute, but he wasn't Lila's type at all. But then, Lila wasn't exactly Todd's type, either. Jessica wasn't sure which of them to feel sorrier for.

"It's too bad couples can't switch partners," she commented to Aaron.

Just then the warning bell rang. Jessica jumped. She had one minute to get to class, and she still didn't know who her husband was. "Uh oh. I've gotta go," she said, rushing off down the hall. She doubled her speed as she turned the corner . . . and collided head-on with Rick Hunter.

"Yikes!" Jessica shrieked as books and papers flew in every direction.

Rick let out a cry of pain and his hand flew to his nose. "Oooowwwww!" he yelled.

"I—I'm sorry," Jessica stammered. "Is it your nose?"

"No," Rick said in a muffled tone. "I'm holding my nose because my ear hurts."

Jessica felt her cheeks flush. It was strange.

Everybody thought Rick Hunter was a really nice guy. He was a seventh grader, very cute and popular, and a great tennis player. But he was always sarcastic with Jessica. He was constantly teasing her and making her feel stupid. She didn't understand it. What had she ever done to Rick?

"You don't have to be sarcastic," she said angrily.

"I do if you're going to ask dumb questions," he shot back.

Jessica began to pick up her books, shoving the papers back into her notebook in no particular order.

"Why are you in such a hurry?" Rick asked as he retrieved his own papers.

Jessica didn't answer.

"Oh, I know," he said. "You're on your way to find out who your 'husband' is." He shook his head sadly. "If I were you, I wouldn't be in such a hurry for the bad news."

"What do you mean?" Jessica demanded.

"You'll find out soon enough."

Jessica's heart sank. It must be somebody really awful.

"Poor Jessica," Rick said.

"Cut it out," Jessica snapped. "I don't even believe you know who it is."

"Oh, I know who it is, all right." He gave a long sigh as he stood up. "Poor Jessica."

"Stop saying that!" she shouted.

Rick looked down at the notebook in his hand. "This is yours," he said, holding it out to her.

Jessica snatched it from his hand and turned on her heel.

"Aren't you even going to thank me?" he asked.

She turned. "Thank you for what? For running into me? For making me drop all my books?"

As Jessica stalked away, she could hear him laughing behind her. She gritted her teeth and kept walking. Rick Hunter was absolutely impossible. And for some reason, Jessica felt as if she could never really defend herself when she was around him. He made her so nervous that she could never seem to get the last word in. Jessica felt sorry for whoever ended up as his wife.

About a dozen kids were gathered in front of the bulletin board where the list was posted. Jessica pushed her way through the crowd and scanned the list, looking for her name.

Her eyes passed over the T's and the U's and the V's. When she got to the W's and found her name, she sucked in her breath with a gasp and felt her heart plummet down into the pit of her stomach.

"Jessica Wakefield," the list read. "Spouse— Rick Hunter."

Three

◇

"Come on, Elizabeth. Please?" Todd was saying as he and Elizabeth hurried to Mr. Seigel's classroom. "Mr. Seigel likes you. If there's one person he'll listen to, it's you. *Everybody* listens to you."

Elizabeth couldn't help feeling flattered. "Thanks, Todd. That's really nice of you to say. But I don't think he's going to change the list just because I ask him to."

"Yeah. But we've probably got a better chance if you ask him than if somebody else asks him."

"I'll try," she said uneasily. "But it doesn't sound all that reasonable to ask Mr. Seigel to change his whole experiment just because we don't like our partners."

"It's not just for us," Todd argued. "Everybody else in the whole middle school is miserable, too."

As Elizabeth and Todd turned the corner and approached Mr. Seigel's classroom, they saw that a group of angry kids was already gathered there. Mr. Seigel stood in the doorway, a harried look on his face.

"No! No, no, no, no. You can't have a divorce," Mr. Seigel said firmly.

"Why not?" Winston Egbert shouted.

"Is this a free country or not?" Dennis Cookman demanded.

"Aren't arranged marriages illegal in the United States?" Maria Slater asked hopefully.

"I think I'm allergic to my partner," Leslie Forsythe put in, wiping her nose with a tissue.

"QUIET!" Mr. Seigel thundered.

The group of students fell silent.

"Now listen to me," Mr. Seigel said sternly. "I don't want to hear any more nonsense about divorce. You haven't even been married an hour."

There were a lot of grumbles from the students. Mr. Seigel held up his hand for silence. "You're just going to have to make the best of things. If you want your marriages to be successful, you're going to have to figure out ways to make them work. This is a very important school project, and I expect you all to work as hard as you can to make it a success."

"Who thought up this stupid project, anyway?" Aaron Dallas demanded.

"I did," Mr. Seigel answered in a frosty tone.

"Oh."

There was an uncomfortable silence.

"But, Mr. Seigel . . ." Kimberly Haver whined.

"No buts. I'll see you all at the third-period assembly. And be sure to show up there with your spouse." With that, Mr. Seigel walked back into his classroom and shut the door with a bang.

Elizabeth turned to Todd and shrugged. "That's that, I guess."

Todd nodded unhappily. "I guess so."

"Well, off to find my husband," Elizabeth said, as the two of them trudged toward their lockers.

Sophia Rizzo hummed happily. It was incredible. It was unbelievable. It was a miracle. She and Patrick Morris had actually been paired in the marriage project.

Patrick was the nicest boy in the whole school. He was smart, too. And considerate. This was going to be a blast.

She rummaged around in her locker. She was about to meet Patrick at the water fountain, and she realized she was feeling a little self-conscious about her appearance. She wished she had worn something today besides her faded jeans and a plain blue oxford shirt. Sophia found the lip gloss Sarah had given her a few weeks ago. She dabbed a little of the light pink color on her lips.

"You're about the happiest-looking person I've seen all morning," she heard a voice say.

Sophia looked up and saw Elizabeth smiling at her. She couldn't help blushing. "You caught me primping," she said with an embarrassed laugh. "Do I look ridiculous?"

"No," Elizabeth said. "You look great. But what's the occasion?"

Sophia straightened the collar on her shirt and smiled. "Guess who I'm married to."

"Who?"

"Patrick Morris," Sophia said with a grin.

"You're kidding."

"I'm not kidding. Isn't that great? We're perfect for each other."

"That *is* great," Elizabeth said. "You really like Patrick. And he really likes you. It's nice that Mr. Seigel got at least one couple matched up right. I think it might be the only one."

"Who are you matched up with?" Sophia asked.

"Mr. Too-Cool-For-School," Elizabeth said unhappily.

"Bruce Patman?" Sophia exclaimed, looking horrified.

Elizabeth nodded.

Yuck! Sophia thought. Bruce was good-looking, but totally conceited. Every time Sophia had ever tried to talk to him, he had interrupted her to brag or show off in some way.

Just then, Patrick walked up. "Ready for class?" he asked, giving Sophia and Elizabeth a smile.

Sophia turned back toward her locker and began to paw through the books and notebooks. "Just as soon as I find my math book."

Patrick leaned patiently against the wall as Sophia searched and searched.

Finally she sighed in frustration. "I can't find it. Never mind. Let's just go to class."

"Look again," Patrick urged. "I'm sure it's there."

"But it's getting late. If I keep looking, I'll make you late for class."

"I don't mind being late for class," Patrick said politely.

"But I don't want you to be late for class because of me."

"I don't want you to have to go without your book because of me," Patrick countered.

"Why don't you go on to class and share Patrick's book?" Elizabeth suggested.

Sophia and Patrick looked at each other. "That's fine with me if it's fine with you," Patrick said.

"Are you sure you don't mind?"

"I don't mind if you don't mind."

"See what I mean?" Sophia whispered happily to Elizabeth. "We're perfect together."

Two hours later, Elizabeth stood outside the auditorium waiting for Bruce. The assembly was about to begin, and Elizabeth had watched couple after couple file in.

Mr. Seigel came by with a stack of project manuals in his hand.

"We're about to start, Elizabeth. You'd better get inside. We've got a lot of important information to go over."

"OK, Mr. Seigel," she said, following him to the doorway.

"Wait a minute." Mr. Seigel stopped and turned to face her. "Where is your spouse?"

"He's not here yet."

Mr. Seigel shook his head. "I'm sorry. But you'll have to wait until he gets here before you take your seat."

"B—but he's not here," Elizabeth protested. "Where is he?"

"I don't know."

"Then you'd better wait for him," Mr. Seigel advised.

"But what if he doesn't get here?"

Mr. Seigel shrugged. "You'll have a big problem."

"But that's not fair. Why should I miss the assembly because of him?"

"You're right. It's *not* fair that you should miss out on something important because he isn't here. So I think that when he does get here, you should discuss that with him. Married partners must be able to rely on one another to live up to their obligations and responsibilities. When one partner fails to do that, the other partner is often penalized."

"But . . . but . . ." Elizabeth sputtered. "That's not fair!" She was too frustrated and confused to think of anything else to say.

"Tell Bruce," Mr. Seigel said calmly. "You were both aware that this is a team effort. He's the one who's letting you down here. Not me."

Mr. Seigel stepped inside the auditorium and firmly shut the door in Elizabeth's face.

Elizabeth stared at the closed door in disbelief. This was horrible. She was here, ready to listen and participate. But she couldn't take part without Bruce. And Mr. Seigel was acting as though it was her responsibility to make sure Bruce was there.

At that moment, Bruce came around the corner.

"Where have you been?" Elizabeth demanded. "The assembly is starting, and Mr. Seigel wouldn't let me in until you showed up."

"Chill out," Bruce answered in a bored tone. "I had business." He smiled. "That's what my dad always says when he's late for something."

Elizabeth let out an impatient sigh. "Your dad isn't doing this project," she snapped. "Now come on, let's get inside."

Bruce rolled his eyes and followed Elizabeth into the auditorium.

Mr. Seigel was already up on the podium giving instructions as Elizabeth and Bruce found two seats together.

"Household budgeting is extremely important," Mr. Seigel was saying. Behind him were several large posters of pie-charts and graphs.

"As part of your assignment, you will be expected to estimate your projected income as a couple and plan accordingly. Behind me, you will see that I have compiled statistics based on national averages with regard to utility costs, housing costs, household expenses, and interest rates. You will be needing this information when you plan your budgets, so please take notes."

Elizabeth opened her notebook and took a pencil from her purse. She noticed that Bruce's notebook remained in his backpack. He wasn't paying a bit of attention. Instead, he was fooling around with his comb, occasionally running it through his hair.

Elizabeth reached over and tapped him on the shoulder. "Aren't you going to take notes?" she whispered.

"We don't both need to take notes," Bruce

answered coolly, leaning back in his seat. "We're a team, remember?"

Elizabeth's pencil moved furiously across her notebook page. But she was so angry at Bruce that she could hardly keep her mind focused on Mr. Seigel's voice.

Mr. Seigel began to circulate the manuals. "One per couple," he reminded them, handing the stack to the nearest student. "By the way, we will have another assembly tomorrow morning. And there will be no fifth period tomorrow afternoon," Mr. Seigel announced. "At fifth period, we will assemble in the cafeteria for a study hall, where you can begin working together on your budgets. I'd like to see preliminary drafts as soon as possible. Final budgets must be submitted in writing at the end of the project. And yes, they will be graded. In fact, every section of this project will be graded."

When the manuals came to Bruce, he didn't even glance at them. He just passed the stack to Elizabeth. Elizabeth took their manual and passed the stack on down the row.

It was clear to Elizabeth that she was going to wind up doing all the work on this project, because Bruce thought the whole thing was too uncool. She sighed. Couldn't Mr. Seigel have put her with someone who was willing to help out at least a little?

* * *

Graded!

Jessica groaned inwardly. She looked over at Rick, who was putting the finishing touches on a very unflattering caricature of her.

That meant she was going to have to really make an effort to do well on this project. She couldn't just blow it off like she'd planned to when she first found out she was married to Rick.

Her grades had been getting worse and worse lately, and her parents had made it clear that if she didn't do something about it, she was going to wind up grounded. In fact, her mother had brought up the subject at breakfast that morning.

She looked down at her notebook. There were some notes about utility costs that didn't even make sense to her now. Mostly the page was covered with doodles and scribbles.

"We'll go broke if you're in charge of anything," Rick whispered.

"What are you talking about?" Jessica demanded.

"You put down a million dollars a month for electricity," he said, laughing.

She looked down at her notebook and frowned in confusion. There did seem to be an awful lot of zeroes on the page.

Her cheeks flushed and she began to erase her mistake.

"Forget about it." Rick grinned. "We're probably going to fail this whole thing anyway."

"I can't afford to fail," Jessica retorted.

"I'll bet you can't," Rick teased. "You airhead types aren't exactly whizzes at school."

"Oh yeah?" Jessica gave him a level stare. "I haven't seen your name on the honor roll lately, either."

"Maybe because you don't know how to spell it."

"I know how to spell your name," Jessica snapped. "B–O–N–E–H–E–A–D!"

Rick threw back his head and laughed. He didn't have a comeback, but he didn't even seem to care. Somehow, that just made Jessica feel more irritated. It was especially annoying to be insulted by somebody who refused to be insulted back.

Mr. Seigel frowned in their direction, and both Rick and Jessica ducked down a little in their seats.

"Don't forget," Mr. Seigel said, just before he dismissed everyone for lunch. "I expect you all to sit with your spouses in the cafeteria. You should take that time to study the materials you have been given and to discuss them."

There was a heavy silence in the auditorium as the students collected their papers and notebooks and began to file out.

"Come on," Rick said. "Let's go straight to the cafeteria. I'm starved."

"I've got to go by my locker first," Jessica said.

"Go by your locker after lunch," Rick said lightly. "If we don't hurry, we'll be last in line."

"I don't want to carry all this stuff to lunch," Jessica argued.

Rick took Jessica's backpack from her. "I'll carry it," he offered. He slung it over his shoulder and headed toward the cafeteria.

Jessica was startled, but pleased. It was nice to have Rick carry her books for her. Maybe it was his way of telling her he wanted to be friends after all. She couldn't help but notice that when he dropped the sarcasm and smiled, he was really cute.

As they approached the door to the cafeteria, Rick scooted ahead and politely held the door for her. For some reason, it made Jessica feel embarrassed. "Th–thank you," she stammered, blushing.

"You're welcome." He smiled at her.

Jessica wasn't sure, but she thought he might be blushing too. She stared at him for a moment, but he quickly turned his head. "Come on. Let's get in line."

Rick handed her a tray, then got one for himself. *Maybe this really isn't going to be so bad,* Jessica thought. She reached out to take a plate of spaghetti.

"You're not going to eat that, are you?" Rick asked innocently.

"Why not?" Jessica asked.

"It'll make you fat," he said with a nasty laugh.

Jessica felt a little stab of worry. Did he think she looked fat? She couldn't be fat. She and Elizabeth were still exactly the same size, and Elizabeth wasn't fat at all.

Her hand automatically reached out and took a soda, just like she did every day.

"You're not going to drink that, are you?" he asked, his voice rising in exaggerated surprise.

Jessica's flicker of worry turned into irritation. "Why not?" she demanded.

"It'll give you pimples," he said. "Then they'll throw you out of the Unicorn Club."

Jessica narrowed her eyes angrily and reached for a piece of garlic bread.

"You're not going to eat that—"

Jessica didn't let him finish. "Yes, I am going to eat this. Why shouldn't I? There's nothing wrong with bread, is there?"

"It's garlic bread. It'll give you bad breath."

Jessica tossed her hair haughtily and picked up her tray. "Why is it any of your business what I have for lunch?"

"I just don't want to be married to somebody fat, pimply, and stinky."

"Oh yeah?" Jessica almost shouted. "Well, I

don't want to be married to somebody who's probably going to be bald by the time he's in tenth grade.'' Jessica picked up her tray and began to walk away.

Rick picked up his own tray and hurried behind her. "I'm never going bald," he protested.

Jessica turned and stared at his hairline. "Oh yeah? Hmmm. The hair on top of your head looks pretty thin to me."

"Speaking of thin, I still think you ought to lay off the pasta."

Jessica turned away angrily. She spotted Lila and Todd sitting over by the window and started in their direction.

"Wait up, airhead," Rick said. "We're supposed to sit together."

"I'm sitting with Lila," Jessica snapped. "I don't care where you sit . . . *bonehead.*"

But Rick followed her anyway.

Jessica's hands were shaking by the time she put her tray down. What had happened? she wondered angrily. What had gone wrong? Five minutes ago they were friends, and now they were trading insults again.

"It's ridiculous," Lila said as soon as Jessica and Rick sat down.

"What's ridiculous?" Rick asked.

"The whole idea of a budget," Lila snapped. "Why should somebody like me have to figure out a budget? I'm never going to have to live on a budget."

"Why not?" Rick asked.

"Because I have a trust fund," Lila said haughtily.

"What's a trust fund?" Rick asked.

"It means she has a lot of money," Jessica said irritably. She wished she had sat down someplace else. It was bad enough that she had to listen to Rick's teasing. Now she had to listen to Lila brag about being rich. Even if Lila's father *was* one of the wealthiest people in Sweet Valley, Jessica was sick of hearing her talk about it.

Rick turned to Jessica. "That sounds pretty good. Do you have a trust fund, Jessica?"

"No," Jessica snapped.

"Gee, that's too bad. No money. And no brains, either. A double washout. Something tells me I lost the lottery of looooove."

Jessica's eyes narrowed dangerously. "You're a loser, all right," she snarled. "But it's not because of me."

She grabbed her tray and stood up. Her appetite was gone and she couldn't stand sitting there another minute.

"I was kidding," Rick said quickly. "Couldn't you tell I was kidding? Where's your sense of humor?"

He threw out his arms in a bewildered

gesture, and when he did, he accidentally whacked his hand into Jessica's arm.

"Hey!" she shouted, losing control of her tray.

She struggled to keep it level, but the heavy tray tipped to the side and spaghetti, soda, and garlic bread came sliding off and splattered in every direction.

Jessica took a quick step backward.

"Look out!" Rick warned.

But it was too late. Jessica's heel came down on a stray piece of tomato, and the next thing she knew, her legs flew out from under her. She came down hard on her behind—right in the middle of the gooey, sticky mess.

Rick stared at her for a moment with his mouth open. Then his face crumpled and his shoulders began to shake with laughter.

The whole cafeteria stood up to see what had happened. Everyone began to laugh and applaud.

"Way to go, Jessica!" Bruce shouted.

Jessica just sat there, her cheeks bright red. She had never felt so humiliated in her whole life. Never. And it was all Rick's fault.

He held out his hand to help Jessica to her feet. But Jessica angrily pushed it away and got up without his help.

"Thanks a bunch," she said coldly, wiping her skirt with the napkins Lila held out to her.

"Better wash that off with water," Todd suggested quietly.

It was all Jessica could do not to run out of the cafeteria, but she forced herself to walk with as much dignity as she could.

"Wait up," she heard Rick shout.

But she didn't wait. She kept walking, wishing she could just walk right out of Sweet Valley Middle School and never come back.

"Would you like some of my french fries, Sophia?"

Sophia smiled at Patrick. He was the nicest boy she'd ever met. She eyed the french fries. They looked good, and she was still hungry. But she'd already eaten two slices of pizza. If she accepted the fries, Patrick might think she ate like a pig.

"No, thank you," she said with a smile. "I'm too full to eat another bite." A strange growling noise came from the direction of her stomach.

Patrick frowned. "Did you hear something?"

"I think it's the garbage disposal in the kitchen," Sophia said, hoping he wouldn't notice her blush. "Would you like my pie?" she offered quickly.

"Don't you want it?" Patrick asked.

Sophia shook her head. "Oh, no. I never eat desserts. I don't even know why I took it."

"I'll take a little piece," Patrick said. "But only if you promise to eat the rest."

He smiled, and Sophia's stomach did a little flip-flop. Suddenly, she really wasn't hungry anymore.

Four

◆

The next day, as Jessica hurried toward the auditorium, she spotted Rick waiting outside the door, tapping his foot impatiently. He smiled when he saw her, and almost in spite of herself, Jessica found herself smiling back. But then Rick's smile turned into a smirk. "It's about time you got here, airhead. I thought maybe you'd forgotten we had an assembly—or else that you'd left me for another man."

"I wish I could, bonehead," Jessica hissed as they hurried into the auditorium and found two seats near the aisle.

"May I have your attention, please?" Mr. Seigel called out.

Jessica glued her eyes to the front of the auditorium, determined to ignore Rick no matter what he said.

Mr. Seigel smiled out at the students. "Congratulations," he said. "You are all about to become parents."

The auditorium erupted into surprised laughter and whispers.

Mr. Seigel clapped his hands. "Quiet, please!"

A hush fell over the auditorium as Mr. Seigel produced a large basket with a cloth over it. When he removed the cloth, several students began to laugh.

Inside the basket were eggs. Lots of eggs. Some of them had pink stickers on them, and some of them had blue stickers.

"Make mine a boy," Aaron Dallas shouted. "Sunny-side up."

Jessica laughed along with the other students, and even Mr. Seigel smiled.

"Okay," he said with a grin. "I'm going to ask each couple to come up on the stage to receive an infant. When you get up here, I'm going to ask you a question. You'll have only a few seconds to discuss the question, and then you must give me an answer. Each couple will be asked a different question."

"Will our answer affect our grade?" Caroline Pearce asked.

"Only if you don't answer the question at

all," Mr. Seigel replied with a smile. "Now then. First couple up: Rick Hunter and Jessica Wakefield."

Rick nudged Jessica's arm. "Let's go," he said.

Jessica nervously got to her feet and followed Rick down the aisle and up the stairs to the stage.

"It's like a game show," Todd Wilkins said loudly.

"What do they win?" Lloyd Benson called out.

Jessica couldn't help laughing, even though she was nervous.

Mr. Seigel selected an egg with a blue sticker. "It's a boy," he said solemnly. "Now the question is, what's his name?"

"That's too easy," Dennis Cookman shouted.

"Settle down," Mr. Seigel warned the students. Then he turned back to Jessica and Rick.

"Let's name it Steven," Jessica suggested to Rick.

"Steven!" Rick groaned. "That's your brother's name. Don't you have any imagination?"

"Well, then, you think of something," Jessica snapped.

"I like Fido," Rick said.

"That's a dog's name."

"Well, I'd rather have a dog than a baby," Rick said with a shrug.

"I'd rather have a dog than a husband," Jessica retorted.

Practically the whole audience burst into laughter except Mr. Seigel.

"Your time is up," Mr. Seigel said. "What's the baby's name?"

"Steven," Jessica answered.

"Fido," Rick said at the same time.

"What was that?" Mr. Seigel asked.

"Steven!" Jessica insisted.

"Fido," Rick argued, laughing.

"I must ask you two to reach a decision. If you don't, your grade will be marked down five points."

Jessica and Rick looked at each other in astonishment. "But that's not fair," Jessica protested.

"Life's not fair," Mr. Seigel answered calmly. "Now please choose a name. If you can't agree, you must compromise."

Jessica opened her mouth and shot a look at Rick, as if daring him to say a word. "His name is Steven," she said firmly. She saw Rick's eyes begin to gleam with mischief. "Steven Fido," she added quickly, before Rick could speak up again and blow things for them both.

The audience roared with laughter and Mr. Seigel smiled. "It's unusual. But each couple is certainly free to choose the name they like best. Steven Fido it is."

Mr. Seigel placed the egg in Jessica's hand. "Now," he said, "Steven Fido is your responsibility. One of you must have him with you at all times, or see to it that he is properly taken care of. I'll expect you to return him intact at the end of the experiment. If he breaks, you will lose five points off your grade."

"Sure you don't want me to hold him, Jessica?" Rick teased. "You know how clumsy you are. Look at the mess you made in the cafeteria yesterday."

"*I* made!" Jessica said. She felt herself gritting her teeth. What had happened in the cafeteria was all *his* fault. He knew it as well as she did. So why was he needling her? Her hand involuntarily balled into a fist and . . .

CRACKKK!

"Eeuuuu," the audience moaned.

Jessica looked down in horror. Runny yellow egg yolk oozed from between her fingers and dripped down onto the stage. Rick burst out laughing, and Mr. Seigel shook his head sadly.

"I—I'm sorry," Jessica stammered, wishing she could just drop right down through a big hole in the stage and never be seen again.

She shot a glance out into the audience and saw Janet and Lila giggling. *It's all Rick's fault,* Jessica thought bitterly. *He made a fool out of me yesterday in the cafeteria. And now he's making a fool out of me in front of the whole school.*

Mr. Seigel reached into his pocket and produced a handkerchief. He handed it to Jessica with a shake of his head. "I'm afraid that's going to shave a few points off of your grade, Jessica."

Jessica nodded unhappily as she wiped the sticky egg off her hands.

"If you're smart," Mr. Seigel said, "you will regard everything in life as a learning experience —even your mistakes. I would say Jessica and Rick have already learned a valuable lesson about parenting."

Jessica and Rick looked at each other in confusion.

"They've learned that when parents bicker and don't learn to control their tempers, the children suffer. Look at what happened to poor little Steven Fido."

Jessica looked over at Rick. Finally, he was looking just as chagrined as she felt. Maybe now he'd quit teasing her and act more responsible.

Mr. Seigel handed a second egg to Rick. "What's his name?"

Rick thought for a moment as Jessica glared at him. "Steven Fido the second," Rick said with a sly grin.

Jessica sighed and rolled her eyes in exasperation. Rick was still Rick.

Sophia Rizzo felt sorry for Jessica as she watched the whole scene. It was too bad she and

Rick had so much trouble getting along. Sophia and Patrick, on the other hand, got along beautifully. They were going to have no trouble at all.

"Okay, next couple," Mr. Seigel called out. He looked down at his sheet. "Sophia Rizzo and Patrick Morris."

Uh oh, Sophia thought. *Here's where we have to prove it.*

"Let's go," Patrick whispered.

Sophia nervously wiped her damp palms on her knees and stood up to follow Patrick.

When they got up onstage, Mr. Seigel very carefully handed Patrick an egg with a pink sticker. "Congratulations. It's a girl."

Sophia and Patrick smiled at each other.

"Now," Mr. Seigel continued, "where do you think she should go to nursery school?"

Sophia looked at Patrick.

Patrick looked at Sophia.

"What do you think?" Sophia whispered.

"Whatever you think is fine with me," Patrick answered.

"Well, I'm happy to go along with whatever you want," Sophia responded.

"You're really smart," Patrick said. "Let's send her wherever you went to nursery school."

"Well, you're smart, too," Sophia said politely. "Where did you go?"

Mr. Seigel clapped his hands. "Sorry. Your time is up. You must give me an answer."

Sophia's mouth felt dry. She was getting a little frustrated. Normally, she'd just speak right up and say she wanted her little girl to go to Sweet Valley Nursery School. But she didn't want Patrick to think she was bossy and opinionated. She wished Patrick would speak up.

But Patrick looked just as indecisive as Sophia felt.

Mr. Seigel shook his head sadly. "Poor little thing. She'll never get to go to nursery school, because her parents can't decide where to send her."

A few of the students laughed.

Sophia felt her cheeks turning red. Patrick looked embarrassed, too.

"Sit down," Mr. Seigel told them. "We have a lot more children to hand out." He looked down at his list. "Janet Howell and Randy Mason."

Sophia and Patrick left the stage and went back to their seats. Sophia felt just miserable, wondering if she'd made a mistake by not speaking up. Now they'd lost a few points off their grade.

Janet Howell hurried past them. Randy had to practically run behind her to catch up.

"Hurry up," Janet ordered. "And let me do the talking," she commanded in a know-it-all voice. "*I* won't have any trouble making decisions."

Patrick nudged Sophia gently. "Boy," he breathed. "I sure am glad I'm not married to Janet. She's horrible."

Sophia swallowed and tried to smile. She didn't blame him. Janet was so bossy she sounded like a monster. Speaking up and saying what was on your mind was a bad idea, Sophia decided. A really, really bad idea.

"This is a U.S. Employment Statistics survey," Mr. Seigel announced, holding up a thick pamphlet. Jessica shifted in her seat as she watched Mr. Seigel start a stack of pamphlets circulating through the cafeteria.

The cafeteria had been turned into a study hall so that all the couples could start working on their budgets. Everyone sat at the long cafeteria tables with their notebooks and calculators.

"This survey lists almost every conceivable kind of job, and the average salary a person in that job can expect to command," Mr. Seigel explained. "Now, most of you probably have some idea of what you might like to do when you grow up. Some of you may want to be doctors. Some of you may want to be electricians. Some of you may want to be graphic designers. Whatever you think you want to be, find the average salary for your profession and plan a budget based on that amount of income."

Rick took a copy of the survey as the stack

went by them, and opened it curiously. "So what do you want to be?"

"An actress on *Days of Turmoil*," Jessica answered promptly. *Days of Turmoil* was her favorite soap opera.

"An actress?" Rick snorted.

"Or a model," Jessica said.

"Well, that's realistic," Rick said sarcastically. He laughed. "If you really want to be a model or an actress, you'd better cut out the sodas and sweets."

Jessica glowered at Rick. "What do you want to be?"

"A rock star."

"Oh, right. That's real practical." Jessica grabbed the survey and quickly flipped to the R's. "So practical there's not even a listing for rock star in here." Jessica waved the employment survey under his nose.

"What would you know about being practical?" he countered. "You're the one who put down a million dollars for electricity in our budget. Gimme that thing."

Rick snatched the survey out of Jessica's hands and began to flip through it. "Try musician," he said. "Here it is. Musician. Seems to me you could have figured that out on your own."

Jessica glared at Rick. Why did he always seem to get the best of her? No matter what she said, he found some way to needle her.

"It doesn't matter what you want to be when you grow up, Rick," she snapped, grabbing the survey back from him. "Because you'll *never* grow up."

"What's the trouble here?" a stern voice demanded.

Jessica looked up guiltily and saw Mr. Seigel standing over her with his hands on his hips.

"Please keep your voice down, Jessica. Some of these people are taking this project seriously. Do them the courtesy of allowing them to work in relative quiet."

Jessica almost felt like crying. It was so unfair. Rick had been teasing her ever since this project started. She'd only been trying to defend herself. And now Mr. Seigel was yelling at *her* when he should have been yelling at Rick.

Mr. Seigel glanced down at the blank sheet of paper in front of her. "Aren't you two making any progress?"

Jessica shook her head.

"Never mind," Mr. Seigel's face relaxed. "Marriage is never easy at first." He looked around. "But where's your baby?"

Rick smiled cheerfully and pointed to his chest. "Right here. In my pocket. Safe and sound."

Mr. Seigel smiled. "It's not the usual place to keep a baby. But as long as it's safe and looked after, that's the most important thing. Carry on. And try to keep your voice down, Jessica."

Mr. Seigel turned away to talk with the couple sitting behind them, and Rick wagged his finger at Jessica. "Yeah, Jessica. Keep your voice down. You might wake the baby. Now let me have the survey. You're obviously not getting anywhere."

Jessica's eyes narrowed angrily. The employment survey was rolled up in her hand like a newspaper.

She'd let him have it, all right. Jessica swung the survey in his direction, whacking him squarely on the chest.

CRACKKK!

Rick looked startled for a second, then began to laugh. He reached into his pocket and removed some dripping pieces of eggshell. "Awww, honey, you smashed the baby."

Mr. Seigel suddenly appeared behind Jessica again and sighed regretfully. "This is not good, Jessica. This is not good at all. Come to my classroom after school and pick up another egg."

"I'm sorry about that," Rick said in a subdued voice when Mr. Seigel walked away. "I didn't mean to make you so mad."

"What do you care?" Jessica asked angrily.

Rick's face looked genuinely unhappy for a moment. But then the familiar grin appeared. "Because this is my favorite shirt."

* * *

Elizabeth hastily erased some figures from the budget she and Bruce were working on. "This is really hard," she said, sighing in frustration. "I thought it would be easy. Sort of like budgeting out my weekly allowance. But it's not the same thing at all. There are so many things to think about. Look at this." She pointed to a column of figures in her notebook.

There was no answer from Bruce.

"Bruce?" Elizabeth said, looking up.

Bruce was doodling in his notebook, a bored look on his face.

"Bruce," Elizabeth said, trying to keep her voice from sounding as angry as she felt. "Mr. Seigel said we're supposed to work on this together. That means you're going to have to help."

Bruce yawned. "Yeah. OK," he agreed casually. "The study hall is almost over. Maybe I can find some time tomorrow. But I don't know how much help I'm going to be. This kind of stuff just isn't my thing."

Elizabeth shook her head. "Then we'll have to get somebody to help us who knows about this stuff. Why don't you come over to my house tonight? We can ask my dad for help."

"You really think your dad is going to help with this?" Bruce asked, his eyebrows lifting in surprise.

"Sure," Elizabeth said. "Why not?"

Five

"Elizabeth!" Mr. Wakefield shouted. "I think your friend is here."

Elizabeth came hurrying down the steps just in time to see her father heading for the front door, wearing an apron and holding a spatula in one hand. When he opened the door, she spotted Bruce Patman standing on the front step.

"Come in," Mr. Wakefield said, reaching out to shake hands with his free hand. "Nice to see you, Bruce."

"Nice to see you, too," Bruce responded automatically. "Are you going to a costume party?"

Mr. Wakefield laughed, looking down at his apron. "No. I just like to cook. Mrs. Wakefield is at a business dinner with some clients tonight, so

I'm taking over the kitchen. She's a part-time designer, and a very talented one," he said proudly. He smiled at Bruce. "Have you eaten?"

Bruce shook his head.

"Great," Mr. Wakefield said. "Then you're just in time for my famous chicken à la Wakefield."

Mr. Wakefield walked to the bottom of the steps. "Steven! Jessica! Dinner."

Steven, the twins' fourteen-year-old brother, appeared at the top of the stairs. He was a freshman at Sweet Valley High, and one of the star players on the JV basketball team. "Hey, Bruce," he said. He turned to Mr. Wakefield. "Jessica went over to Rick Hunter's house. They're working on some school project."

"Oh, that's right," Mr. Wakefield said. "She told me this afternoon." He turned to Elizabeth. "I guess it's the same project you and Bruce are working on."

Mr. Wakefield headed back toward the kitchen. "Steven, why don't you help me get the plates? And Elizabeth, will you set a place for Bruce?"

"Sure," Elizabeth said.

Bruce turned to Elizabeth with a confused expression on his face. "Your dad really cooks?" he whispered.

Elizabeth grinned. "Sure. My dad can do anything."

* * *

"Yeah! Yeah!" Bruce nodded enthusiastically. "I see exactly what you mean."

Elizabeth had a hard time keeping herself from laughing. Somewhere in the last two hours, Bruce Patman seemed to have forgotten that he was too cool for the marriage project.

At first, Bruce had seemed a little bored and distant when Mr. Wakefield had started to explain things. But it wasn't long before he began to respond to Mr. Wakefield. Actually, Elizabeth wasn't surprised. Her dad was warm and friendly, and he was great at explaining things.

Bruce smacked his forehead. "I can't believe I was so dumb," he groaned. "It's really simple."

Mr. Wakefield nodded. "It takes a while to get a feel for budgeting," he said. "If you just look at it as a math problem, it gets simpler. And you seem to have a good grasp of math."

"You think so?" Bruce asked happily. "Sometimes I think I like it. But then sometimes it seems frustrating and boring."

Mr. Wakefield laughed. "Lots of things in life seem frustrating and boring at first," he said. "But if you persevere and are committed, you discover that it stops being frustrating and boring, and becomes very rewarding. Law school seemed frustrating and boring at first, but it was well worth the effort. I'm a lawyer now and I love what I do. Steven thought basketball was frustrating, too. Now he's a very good player."

His face was suddenly serious. "This is a very worthwhile project," he said to Elizabeth and Bruce. "Marriage and children aren't easy. But it's just like everything else in life—law school, basketball—the more you put into it, the more you get out of it. And there's nothing in the world more important than your family."

Bruce nodded solemnly.

Just then Steven walked into the living room. "Hey, Dad, you still want to practice some jump shots?"

Mr. Wakefield looked at Bruce and Elizabeth. "Can you two work along on your own for a while?" he asked. "I did promise Steven I'd get in some hoop time with him tonight." He patted his stomach. "Besides, I can use the exercise."

"Sure," Elizabeth said.

"You bet," Bruce agreed.

Bruce watched as Mr. Wakefield left the living room. "Your dad is unbelievable," he said, turning to Elizabeth with a serious expression.

Elizabeth smiled. She was proud of her dad, but she had never exactly thought of him as unbelievable. "What do you mean?"

"I mean it's really cool how he spends time with you. How he does things around the house. Cooking. Helping you with homework. Playing basketball with Steven."

"Doesn't your dad do stuff like that?" Elizabeth asked.

Bruce shook his head. Elizabeth thought he looked a little sad. "My dad travels a lot," he said. "He's usually so busy that he leaves the house and kids stuff to my mom."

Elizabeth nodded, finding it a little strange to be having such a serious conversation with Bruce Patman.

Bruce bit his lip and frowned. "I like my dad. I really like him a lot. But I don't see him that much. If I ever do get to be a father, I'd like to be like your dad. You know—involved and everything."

"You made a good start tonight," Elizabeth said encouragingly. "Once my dad explained how to do the budget, you practically did the whole thing."

Actually, Bruce had really taken over the whole thing. But Elizabeth didn't want to criticize him for it. It was better than having him do nothing.

Bruce nodded. "If you don't mind," he said thoughtfully, "I think I'll take home the manual Mr. Seigel gave us. It probably wouldn't be a bad idea to look it over. I'm going to give this thing my best shot." He smiled at her. "From now on, I'm a family man."

* * *

Elizabeth had just changed into her night-gown when she heard the door to Jessica's room slam.

A few seconds later, Jessica came stomping through the bathroom that connected their rooms, and stood in Elizabeth's doorway.

"What's wrong?" Elizabeth asked, noticing Jessica's angry face.

"Rick Hunter is a total jerk!" Jessica shouted. She waved some pages of loose-leaf paper in the air. "Listen to this. Rick told me to read over the manual and take notes while he did the budget. Two hours later, *this* is what he came up with. It's a joke. Look at what he put in the 'necessity' column."

Elizabeth looked at the budget and began to laugh. "A two-story atrium for snakes!"

Jessica waved another piece of paper in Elizabeth's face. "And look at this!"

Elizabeth's eyes widened as she ran her eyes down the sheet. Poor Jessica. The budget was a total mess. There was money put aside for motorcycles, para-sailing lessons, and concert tickets, but none for food, rent, or baby expenses.

Elizabeth couldn't help laughing.

"It's not funny," Jessica fumed.

"Yes it is," Elizabeth countered. "Actually, I think you and Rick are the perfect couple. This is exactly the kind of budget *you'd* put together."

Jessica gave her a grudging smile. "Yeah. It

is. Except that I know that's not the kind of budget Mr. Seigel wants to see. And I've *got* to get a decent grade."

Jessica turned to go back into her room. "Looks like I'm going to be up all night. Mr. Seigel said he wanted to see preliminary budgets tomorrow. I guess that means I'm going to have to figure out how to do a budget whether I like it or not."

Sophia Rizzo swung her backpack happily as she came up the street on her way to school on Thursday morning. Patrick Morris had come over for dinner the night before and they had worked all evening on their budget.

She turned the corner that led to Sweet Valley Middle School and was startled to see Jessica Wakefield sitting on the wall in front of the school building.

Jessica was furiously punching buttons on her calculator and scribbling with a pencil.

"What are you doing here so early?" Sophia asked.

Jessica looked up, and Sophia noticed that her eyes looked tired. "I'm trying to finish up this budget." She hastily erased a figure and corrected it.

"How come Rick's not helping you?"

"Because Rick is no help at all," Jessica responded angrily. "He won't be serious about this, and I just can't afford to fail. I'm on grounding alert after my last report card."

"But you're supposed to work on it together," Sophia pointed out.

Jessica gave her a frustrated look. "I know we're supposed to do it together. But if I want it done right, I'm going to have to do it myself." She sighed. "I guess your budget is all finished, huh?"

Sophia felt a little flutter of worry in her stomach. "Not exactly," she said.

"How come?" Jessica asked. "I'm sure Patrick doesn't want to spend all your money on stupid stuff like snake houses."

"Not exactly," Sophia said again.

"So what's the problem?" Jessica asked, finally looking up.

Sophia stared at Jessica, debating whether or not to talk to her about Patrick. She and Jessica weren't exactly close—not like Sophia and Elizabeth. But Jessica was a Unicorn, and Unicorns supposedly knew a lot about boys.

"Well, Patrick and I don't *disagree* on anything," she began.

"That's good—isn't it?"

"Well," Sophia said uncertainly, "we're so busy trying not to disagree, we never get around to agreeing."

"What are you talking about?"

"If I ask him how much he thinks we should

allot for car payments, he asks how much *I* think we should allot for car payments."

"So put down what you want."

Sophia shrugged her shoulders irritably. "But what if it's not what he wants?"

Jessica gave Sophia a long look. "Are you feeling OK, Sophia?"

Sophia's eyebrows lifted in surprise. "What do you mean?"

"Well, um, you've always seemed like the . . . uh . . . *outspoken* type."

"You mean I'm a bossy loudmouth?"

"Sort of. In a *good* way, though. You say what you think. Kind of like Janet Howell, except you're not quite as bossy as *that*."

Sophia remembered the way Janet had sounded when she spoke to Randy, and it made her cringe inside. No way did she want to sound like Janet.

Sophia blushed and looked embarrassed. "Oh, forget it. Let's talk about something else. Give me that," she said gruffly, snatching the budget from Jessica. "Maybe I can help."

"It's probably a mess." Jessica sighed gloomily. "I'm not very good at math."

"Are you kidding?" Sophia whistled. "This is great. You've covered all your expenses and you've even put some in a savings account."

"Do you really think it looks OK?"

Sophia handed the budget back to Jessica. "It looks terrific. How'd you do it?"

"I don't know. I guess I just figured out how to do it because . . . because . . ." She couldn't help laughing. "Because I couldn't get anybody to do it for me."

Jessica hurried toward Mr. Seigel's classroom. Now that she felt pretty confident about the budget, she was actually looking forward to class.

And maybe Rick would be so impressed with her that he'd stop calling her airhead.

Jessica smiled. It would be nice if they could be friends. In spite of being such a jerk, Rick *was* awfully cute. If he wanted to call a truce, she wouldn't mind a bit. She'd even forgive him for not helping with the budget.

The final bell rang and Jessica ran the last few feet down the hall. Mr. Seigel wasn't very patient with people who were late for class.

Jessica turned the corner and zoomed into the classroom.

"You're late, Jessica," Mr. Seigel said sharply.

"I'm sorry," she said breathlessly. Out of the corner of her eye, she could see Rick sitting close to the front. There was an empty desk next to him.

Jessica quickly moved toward the empty seat. "It won't happen again," she promised, realizing she'd said the exact same thing the day before.

Just as she began to sit down, Rick lurched forward. "Hold it," he said suddenly.

She froze, her knees bent halfway.

"Don't sit there," he warned.

Jessica drew in her breath. It was bad enough that he didn't want to work on the budget with her. Now he didn't even want to *sit* with her. Well, that was just tough. She threw him a defiant look and sat down.

CRACKKK!

Rick's face fell and there was a sudden hush in the room. Every pair of eyes turned toward Mr. Seigel, and he spun around to face her. "Did I hear what I thought I heard?"

Rick's face crumpled, and he began to make strange wheezing noises. Then he began to laugh. "Awwwww, honey," he choked out. "You sat on the baby."

The entire classroom erupted into laughter, and even Mr. Seigel looked amused.

Wordlessly, he went over to the refrigerator in the back of the science room and removed another egg. Then he walked over and handed it to Jessica.

"Steven Fido the third," Maria Slater said with a laugh.

"No. It's Steven Fido the fourth," Dennis Cookman corrected.

Jessica was so humiliated that she could hardly move. She stared straight ahead, wishing she could just disappear. This was the worst moment of her whole life. Her skirt was ruined. Her life was ruined. She was a total laughingstock. And it was all Rick Hunter's fault.

Six

◇

"I hate Rick Hunter," Jessica said for about the four-thousandth time. The twins were sitting on Elizabeth's bed. It was late Sunday morning, and Jessica had been complaining about Rick all weekend.

Jessica reached out and grabbed Elizabeth's pillow. "I hate him. I hate him. I hate him," she chanted, punching her fist into the pillow.

Elizabeth laughed. "Stop it. That's my favorite pillow," she protested.

"I just wish it were Rick Hunter," Jessica said through gritted teeth. She shook her head. "When Mr. Seigel first announced this project, I kept hoping I wouldn't get stuck with a geek, but now I really wish I had. Rick Hunter is much worse than any geek."

"You used to think he was cute," Elizabeth pointed out.

"*Used to* is right," Jessica muttered, punching the pillow again. "He's totally irresponsible. He refuses to take anything seriously. And I wind up doing all the work. How would you like to be in my shoes?"

Elizabeth reached over and snatched the pillow away from Jessica. "Believe me, I've been in your shoes," she said. "Now you're in mine."

Jessica gave her a blank look. "What are you talking about?"

"*You* are usually totally irresponsible. *You* usually refuse to take anything seriously. And whenever we're working on something together, *I* wind up doing all the work."

"That's not true," Jessica argued.

"Yes it is," Elizabeth insisted.

"Name one time."

Elizabeth took a deep breath. "When we were making dinner last night, when we were doing the dishes after breakfast this morning, when we were—"

Jessica held up her hand and grinned sheepishly. "OK, OK. Let's not argue. You have to help me figure out what to do about Rick."

Elizabeth shook her head in bewilderment. "I just don't understand why you let him get you so rattled. You usually have no trouble sticking up for yourself."

Jessica clutched her fingers more tightly over her face. "Arghhhhh," she groaned.

"I mean, why don't you just tell him to leave you alone?"

Jessica flopped down and moaned into the blanket. "Because."

"Because what?" Just then Elizabeth jumped at the sound of the doorbell. "Are you expecting anybody?" she asked.

Jessica shook her head.

"Neither am I," Elizabeth said.

"Well, you'd better get it," Jessica said in a muffled voice. "Because Mom and Steven are out, and Dad's at the office, and I'm never getting out of bed again as long as I live."

"Hi, Bruce," Elizabeth said. "What's up?"

Bruce stepped into the living room carrying a brown paper grocery bag. He cleared his throat. "OK," he said briskly. "I've read the manual Mr. Seigel gave us—twice. And I made a list of all the things a husband and father is supposed to do." He took a piece of paper from his shirt pocket and consulted it.

"Budget, check. Reading, check. Now I think it's time I spent some time with the children." He folded the paper and put it back in his pocket.

Elizabeth blinked. "You mean our egg?"

"Come on, Elizabeth," Bruce said impatiently. "I'd appreciate some cooperation here. You've got to start taking this thing a little more seriously if you want to get anything out of it. From now on, let's try to believe the egg is a baby."

Bruce reached into his brown paper bag and pulled out a little carrier made out of a shoe box. He had glued straps to either side of it, and covered the bottom with crumpled tissue paper. "I made it myself," he said proudly. "If you don't mind, since you had the baby all last week, I think I'll take him this week. You know, do the bonding thing. See what it's like to be responsible for somebody else."

Bruce's eyes darted around the room, then focused on something sitting on the bookcase. "Ah hah!" he shouted.

Elizabeth jumped.

Bruce dashed toward the bookcase. "I had a feeling something like this might happen. The manual said that it's almost impossible to anticipate all the things that can go wrong if fathers don't stay on their toes." He picked up the egg and cradled it possessively in his palm. "I sure am surprised at you, Elizabeth. How could you leave the baby lying around like that? Don't you realize how fragile it is? That seems pretty irresponsible."

Elizabeth's mouth fell open. "Irresponsible! Me?"

Bruce turned. And as he did, one of the straps on the shoe-box carrier came unglued and the carrier dangled over his arm, swinging from the remaining strap.

"Darn!" Bruce exclaimed. "Now how am I going to carry the baby?"

"Put it in your pocket," Elizabeth suggested. "That's where Rick keeps his and Jessica's egg."

"In my pocket! Are you crazy? Are you *completely* irresponsible?" Bruce demanded.

That did it. Elizabeth knew that if there was one thing she wasn't, it was irresponsible. "I am *not* irresponsible," Elizabeth argued. "I told you the egg—"

"*Baby*," Bruce corrected.

"The *baby* was perfectly safe sitting on the—"

"Now, Elizabeth," Bruce interrupted, "if you had read the manual on parenting and—"

"How could I read the manual when you took it and kept it all week?" Elizabeth sputtered.

But Bruce wasn't listening. "Parenting is the ultimate responsibility," he said, sounding like he was quoting directly from the manual.

"What makes you the big responsibility expert?" Elizabeth demanded.

"I read the manual," Bruce explained simply. "Do you have a stapler?" he asked. "I'd like to repair the carrier."

Elizabeth opened her mouth to argue with him, but then changed her mind. What was the point? He wasn't listening to a word she said.

"Give me that," she said angrily, snatching the egg and the carrier from Bruce. "I'll fix it. There's a stapler in the kitchen."

"Careful," Bruce warned as she stomped out of the living room.

The swinging door that led to the kitchen shut behind her, and Elizabeth went over to the kitchen counter, where her mother had left some business papers and a stapler. Elizabeth sat the egg on the counter and quickly punched a couple of staples into the shoe-box carrier.

She swung it just a bit to be sure the handles were on securely. As she did, the carrier swung out and gently tapped the egg.

In front of her horrified eyes, the egg began to roll toward the edge of the counter.

"No," she whispered, momentarily frozen. "No. No. No."

Elizabeth dropped the carrier and dove toward the egg. But she was a split second too late.

SPLATTTTT!

Elizabeth drew in her breath with a gasp and stared down at the mess on the floor. Yellow egg yolk oozed toward her foot.

"Is it fixed?" she heard Bruce shout from the living room.

Elizabeth felt her face growing pale. If Bruce

found out about this, he'd freak out. He'd accuse her of being irresponsible again. And this time, he'd be right.

Elizabeth nudged a piece of broken shell with her toe. The little pink sticker was still intact.

She looked quickly over her shoulder to make sure no one was watching. Then she bent over and peeled the sticker off the eggshell.

Very carefully, she tiptoed over to the refrigerator and looked inside. On the second shelf from the bottom, there was a bowl of eggs.

She removed an egg from the bowl and pasted the pink sticker onto the shell. Her nails smoothed the edges of the sticker down flat, and she breathed a sigh of relief.

Perfect. Absolutely perfect. Nobody would ever know it wasn't the same egg. And most important, Bruce would never know the difference.

"Do you like spaghetti?" Sophia asked.

"Do you?" Patrick countered.

"Yes. But if you'd rather fix something else, that's fine with me."

It was Monday afternoon, and Sophia and Patrick were in the Sweet Valley Supermarket shopping for the meal they were supposed to prepare in the home-economics kitchen. Each couple had been assigned kitchen time at the school and given a voucher to present to the checker at the grocery store. Then the grocery store would collect the money from the school.

In order to complete the assignment, Sophia and Patrick had to plan a meal, prepare it, eat it, and clean it up. And they had to do it together.

It had all sounded so easy when they talked about it in assembly. But it wasn't turning out to be easy at all. In fact, it was turning out to be just as hard as planning the budget.

"If you want spaghetti," Patrick said cheerfully, "then spaghetti it is." He reached up and took a package of spaghetti noodles off the shelf.

"Wait!" Sophia said.

Patrick's hand hovered uncertainly.

Sophia chewed her lip. Patrick didn't sound all that enthusiastic about spaghetti. Maybe he was just going along with her suggestion because he thought that's what she wanted to make. Maybe he didn't really like spaghetti at all. Maybe she should say she didn't really want to make spaghetti. That way he could feel free to make a suggestion of his own.

"Let's not make spaghetti," she said. "Mr. Seigel might think it's too easy."

Patrick nodded. "You're right. Since our budget is already overdue, we should try as hard as we can on the meal preparation."

Sophia wished he hadn't mentioned the budget. They were still trying to put one together. But at the rate they were going, they'd *never* get it finished.

"Maybe we should make pork chops," Patrick suggested. "That is, if you like pork chops."

Yuck! Sophia thought. She hated pork chops. A big picture of a pan of pork chops filled her mind. She hated the way they looked. She hated the way they smelled. And most of all, she hated the way they tasted.

"I love pork chops," she chirped. "So if you like pork chops and I like pork chops, let's make pork chops."

Patrick studied her face carefully. "Are you sure you're not just saying you like pork chops because I like pork chops? Because if you really don't like pork chops, we don't have to make them."

This is impossible, Sophia thought unhappily. *How can two people who like each other as much as we do have such a hard time making a decision?* She was ready to scream with frustration.

"So what do you think?" Patrick asked.

She drew in her breath. She couldn't stand it anymore. *I think I'm going to scream if you don't make a decision!* she wanted to shout at the top of her lungs.

But then she noticed Patrick's worried frown, and forced herself to smile. "You know, we don't have to get the food today. Our assigned kitchen time isn't until Wednesday. Maybe we should think it over and come back another time. What do you think?"

"Sure. I guess that would probably be the best thing," Patrick said. "What do *you* think?"

Seven

◇

Jessica pushed a grocery cart up the canned-food aisle as Rick followed her.

Rick grabbed a couple of cans off of the shelf. "How about some of this?" He studied the cans carefully. "It says here that this product is an economical and nutritious meal guaranteed to contain all the essential vitamins and minerals." He showed her the cans with a pleased smile.

Jessica rolled her eyes. "It's dog food."

"Yeah. But think how much little Steven Fido would enjoy it."

"Ha ha. Very funny."

Rick put the cans back on the shelf. "Where is little Steven Fido, anyway?"

Jessica pointed to the roomy side pocket of

her purse. "In here. He's fine as long as I'm careful with my purse." She gave the cart a push, turning the corner of the aisle.

"How about making frozen pizzas?" Rick suggested.

"Get serious."

"OK. How about microwave hot dogs?"

Jessica stopped the cart and stamped her foot. "Would you *please* stop joking around? If we don't plan a nutritious, well-balanced meal, Mr. Seigel is going to flunk us."

"Frozen pizza is very nutritious," Rick insisted. "Hey, look at these." Rick grabbed a bag of bright gum balls off the shelf and threw them into the cart. "For dessert," he said with a grin.

Jessica reached into the cart, grabbed the bag of gum balls, and flung them back onto the shelf. "Gum balls don't even qualify as food," she said angrily. "If you'd read any of the information Mr. Seigel gave us, you'd know that."

Rick blew out his breath. "Why are you taking this stuff so seriously?" he asked. "Why can't we have some fun while we're doing this?"

"Because your idea of fun is for us to flunk this project," Jessica snapped. She tossed her hair over her shoulder angrily and began pushing the cart over to the pasta section. "How about macaroni and cheese?" she suggested. "That's economical and nutritious."

There was no answer from Rick.

"Rick?" she prompted.

Silence.

Jessica turned. "Rick?"

Rick was nowhere to be seen.

Jessica sighed. It looked as though she was going to end up doing all the work on this part of the project, too.

She wheeled the cart toward the produce section. A salad would be good with macaroni and cheese. And it would be easy to make.

As she passed the dairy counter, the cartons of eggs caught her eye.

Of course. Egg custard. Why hadn't she thought of that before? It would make a great dessert, and she'd seen her mother prepare it lots of times.

Jessica reached out and picked up a carton of eggs. She'd have to remember to ask her mom for the recipe. She was still staring down thoughtfully at the carton in her hand when suddenly . . .

"BOO!"

Rick jumped out from behind the counter.

Jessica gasped in startled surprise. Her hand opened and the carton began to fall.

"Oh no!" she cried as the entire carton of eggs fell to the floor and exploded into a mess of broken shells and sticky slop.

Jessica could only stand there in appalled silence. Rick's eyes opened wide and he didn't make a sound for a moment.

An angry-looking store clerk came hurrying in their direction. Jessica felt her face turning white.

"All right, young lady," he began, frowning. "If you're one of the Sweet Valley Middle School students, I'm going to need your name."

Jessica's heart began to pound. Now she was really in trouble. She wet her lips nervously. "I'm . . . uh . . . Jessica—"

"It wasn't her fault," Rick said quickly, before she could finish. "It was my fault."

The clerk put his hand on his hips. "I'm supposed to report any kids who are causing trouble."

Rick's jaw jutted forward. "Then report me. I'm Rick Hunter. I'm in the seventh grade. I was fooling around, and it was my fault she dropped the eggs. I'm sorry. I'll clean it up if you'll show me where to find a mop."

Jessica stared at Rick in amazement. She couldn't believe it. He was actually sticking up for her.

The clerk nodded. "OK, Rick. Come with me and I'll find you a mop."

Rick took a second carton of eggs and placed it in Jessica's cart. "Finish the shopping," he said quietly. "I'll meet you at the checkout counter."

Jessica nodded, but didn't say anything. She

suddenly felt too shy to speak. Fortunately, she didn't have to. Rick turned and followed the clerk to the back of the store.

What in the world had made him stick up for her like that? Jessica wondered. It was really nice. It was really responsible. It was so unlike him! Maybe he was reforming.

Jessica shook her head and hurried toward the produce section. She picked out a head of lettuce, a couple of tomatoes, some celery, and an avocado.

Maybe this meant that Rick was going to quit making her life miserable. Maybe he'd quit calling her names and teasing her about every little thing she did or said.

She hurried around the store, finding the last few things they would need to prepare their meal. By the time she got to the checkout counter, she was feeling so happy, she was humming.

Rick was standing at the checkout counter, waiting for her. "Did you get everything?" he asked in a friendly voice.

She nodded shyly and began to take the things out of the cart.

"Let me do that," he said, reaching out to help her.

"Thanks." She smiled.

"It's the least I can do," he said. "After all, you did all the shopping." He carefully placed each item on the conveyor belt. "I'm sorry I almost got you into trouble," he said, avoiding Jessica's eyes and studying the bag of noodles as it rolled past him.

It was funny. It was almost like Rick was feeling shy now.

"That's OK," Jessica said quickly. "I hope you won't get into any trouble."

Rick shrugged. "I don't care if I get into trouble. I guess I'm used to it."

"I always seem to be in trouble, too," Jessica said truthfully.

"I guess that's what makes us a good couple," Rick said with a laugh.

His eyes looked so friendly and happy that Jessica began to laugh, too.

"What are we laughing about?" Rick finally asked.

"I don't know." Jessica giggled.

The cashier efficiently rang up their purchases and totaled them.

"Are you from Sweet Valley Middle School?" he asked.

Rick nodded.

"Great. All I need is for you to give me your voucher."

"Uh, OK." Rick put his hand to his shirt pocket. His face fell. "Oh, no."

"What's the matter?" Jessica asked.

Rick's hands patted the pockets on his shirt

and rifled the pockets of his pants. "Oh, no," he said again.

Jessica had a feeling she knew what was wrong.

"I lost the voucher," Rick said with a little laugh.

"You lost it?"

Rick threw back his head and laughed again. "Yeah. Pretty funny, huh? Oh well, you can ask Mr. Seigel for another one tomorrow. Then you can run over here after school tomorrow and get the groceries."

Jessica glared at him in disbelief. "*I* can ask Mr. Seigel for another one?" she repeated. "*I* can stop by here on my way home from school tomorrow? Why can't *you* ask Mr. Seigel for another one? Why can't *you* stop here after school tomorrow?"

"I've got basketball practice tomorrow," Rick said.

"I've got a Unicorn meeting tomorrow," Jessica responded. Actually, she didn't. But it really irritated her that Rick expected *her* to go to a lot of trouble when *he* was the one who had lost the voucher.

"Basketball's important," Rick said. "The Unicorns aren't. They're just a bunch of silly girls who sit around gossiping."

Suddenly, Jessica was so mad she couldn't

see straight. "Look, bonehead!" she shouted, slamming her purse down on the counter.

CRACKKK!!

Jessica closed her eyes. "Oh, no," she wailed. She opened her eyes again to watch the egg yolk ooze out of the side pocket of her purse onto the counter.

Suddenly the same clerk appeared behind them and lifted his arms in exasperation. "What have you kids got against eggs?" he demanded.

Elizabeth tapped her foot impatiently as she watched Bruce study their shopping list, carefully ticking off each item with a pencil.

"We have everything, Bruce. I checked," she said, trying not to sound as irritated as she felt.

Bruce nodded absently. "Um hum." But he continued checking the list.

"I said I checked it," Elizabeth repeated impatiently.

There was no response from Bruce. Didn't he *ever* listen to anything she said?

Elizabeth furrowed her brows. It was truly weird. Bruce Patman, who had wanted absolutely nothing to do with the project, suddenly seemed determined to take over the whole thing. She was glad he wanted to get involved, but the way he was doing it made her furious.

"If I say I checked the shopping list, I checked it. We have everything," she said angrily.

"Of course," Bruce said in a soothing voice. "I just want to take one last little . . . ah hah!"

"Ah hah *what*?" Elizabeth asked irritably.

"You forgot to get broccoli."

"I did not *forget* to get broccoli. I looked at the broccoli and it was too expensive. So I got squash."

Bruce gave her a patronizing smile. "It's OK if you forgot. You don't have to make up excuses. I forget things, too, sometimes."

"I am *not* making up excuses," Elizabeth stated. "I looked at the broccoli. It was too expensive. I got squash instead. You were getting the hamburger meat, so I made the decision myself."

Bruce gave a little laugh. "I don't know why it's so hard for you to admit you did something wrong."

Elizabeth opened her mouth to argue, but she felt her face turning beet-red as she remembered the broken egg. OK, so maybe it was hard for her to admit it when she did something wrong. But that was because Bruce was determined to be so right about everything. There was no way she could admit she'd broken the egg now—she'd never hear the end of it.

"Oh, forget it," she grumbled. "Let's just get out of here." She began to take the groceries out of the cart.

"Be careful not to bruise the fruit," Bruce said helpfully.

Elizabeth picked up two peaches and practically slammed them on the counter.

Bruce shook his head. "You know, Elizabeth, I never realized what a bad temper you have. That's something you should really work on. I read in the manual that children can react very negatively to adult displays of temper. In fact, the manual said that . . ."

I wish I'd never given him that manual, Elizabeth thought. *I've created a monster!*

Sophia heard the phone as soon as she opened the kitchen door. She threw down her books and picked up the extension in the kitchen. "Hello?"

"Jerry McAllister is the worst husband in the whole world," Sarah Thomas squeaked in indignation. "He argues with everything I say. It took us *two hours* to do the shopping for our meal. Now we're not even speaking."

"Sounds awful, Sarah," Sophia said.

"And he's an incredible klutz, too," Sarah went on. "It seems like he's always stepping on my toes or knocking me into something. I don't know what made me think this project was going to be romantic. It's the pits!"

Sophia sighed gloomily. "I tried to tell you."

There was a long pause from Sarah's end. "What's the matter with *you*? I thought *your* marriage was working out great. You said you and Patrick were the perfect couple."

"We are. We're so perfect and polite that we can't get anything done."

"Polite, *you*?" Sarah said with a laugh.

"Believe it or not, yes." Sophia sighed again.

"Quit sighing," Sarah said. "It's such a depressing sound."

"I can't help it," Sophia said. "I am depressed. I have the perfect husband, and I just wish I had somebody I could yell at."

Mrs. Rizzo came hurrying into the kitchen that evening with her arms full of groceries and files from work. "Such a day," she said in her lightly accented English. She kissed Sophia on the cheek. "How was school? How is your marriage project coming along?"

Sophia finished drying the dishes she had been washing and fidgeted with the dish towel. "I'm glad you asked, Mama. Because I really need to ask you something."

"Ask, ask," Mrs. Rizzo said with a smile. Sophia noticed how pretty her mom looked when she smiled. In fact, she seemed to be smiling all the time these days—ever since she'd started going out with Mr. Thomas. "What do you want to know?"

"Am I bossy?"

"Sometimes, yes," Mrs. Rizzo answered.

"But that is because you are a Rizzo. We are all bossy, I'm afraid. You. Tony. Especially me," she finished with a laugh.

That was true, Sophia reflected. Her mother could really lay down the law when she needed to. She could stick to her guns, too. If she thought something wasn't fair, she spoke right up. Sophia had seen her do it lots of times. So maybe Sophia should start speaking up around Patrick. Say what was on her mind. Express her opinions and quit worrying about what he thought.

Just then the phone rang and Mrs. Rizzo reached for the extension. "Hello? . . . Oh yes, *hello*," she said happily.

Sophia could tell from her mother's voice that it was Mr. Thomas.

"What? Tonight? . . . I would love to . . . Yes." Mrs. Rizzo smiled. "Chinese food sounds wonderful . . . uh huh . . . All right then, I will see you at eight." She said good-bye and hung up the phone.

Chinese food sounds wonderful! Sophia's jaw dropped. "But Mama, you hate Chinese food," she said.

"Yes. But Mr. Thomas loves it. And sometimes, it's necessary to compromise. It's all part of the give and take of relationships, Sophia. Now, what was it you were asking me?"

"Never mind," Sophia said gloomily.

Eight

Elizabeth lifted the top of a pot to check the rice.

"Not yet," Bruce said, firmly replacing the top. "The recipe said to keep the pot covered tightly until the cooking time is up."

Elizabeth sighed and went over to the oven. If Bruce wouldn't let her look at the rice, she could at least check on the hamburger patties that were under the broiler.

Bruce and Elizabeth were in the home-economics kitchen. Bruce had signed them up for the first time available, and he was determined that their meal was going to be the best.

"Don't open that," Bruce warned. "If you keep opening the oven, you change the level of heat inside. It messes up the cooking time."

"Can't I do something?" Elizabeth asked irritably.

"You just relax," Bruce said encouragingly. "I've got everything under control."

"I'll peel the peaches," she offered.

"I've already done it."

"OK. Then I'll steam the squash."

"It's already in the steamer."

Elizabeth let out her breath in an impatient gasp. "Well, what am I supposed to do?"

"You could converse about current events, or books you've enjoyed reading."

Elizabeth rolled her eyes. He was quoting from the manual again.

Bruce edged past her with a handful of silverware. "I really liked that chapter in the manual about family mealtimes. You know, a lot of that stuff made sense. Family members *should* make an effort to sit down together at least once a day to have a meal and share their thoughts. I'm sure your dad always makes time for family meals."

Bruce took the shoe-box carrier from the counter and carefully placed it on a chair at the table. "Children are never too young to be included in important family gatherings," he said seriously.

Oh, brother, Elizabeth thought. *Another quote from the manual.*

Elizabeth got some napkins out of the drawer and set them in the middle of the table.

Bruce frowned. "Not like that. The picture of the table in the manual showed the napkins folded up at each place."

Elizabeth reached for the napkins and grudgingly began to fold them. Actually, her mother always insisted that napkins be folded, too. But there was just something about Bruce's by-the-book attitude that made her feel like rebelling.

Suddenly she had a sinking feeling that this was exactly how Jessica felt when Elizabeth was being a perfectionist. *But I couldn't possibly be as bad as Bruce*, she told herself.

She took two water glasses out of the cabinet and set them on the left side of each place.

"On the right. On the right," Bruce instructed. "If you'd studied the place settings like I did, you'd know that water glasses go on the right. Salad bowls go on the left."

Elizabeth felt like strangling him. What a know-it-all. And the worst part of it was, he wasn't *trying* to be a know-it-all, he was trying to be nice.

"I like my water glass on the left," she said stubbornly, setting each glass down on the left side of the plate. She made a mental promise to let Jessica set the table however she wanted to from now on.

Bruce wagged his finger. "Tsk tsk. Come on,

Elizabeth. There's a right way to do things and a wrong way." He firmly moved each glass to the right.

"Sometimes I'd rather do things the wrong way than the right way," she said, moving the glasses back to the left.

Bruce looked angry for a moment, but then he took a deep breath and gave her a serene smile. "You're just feeling cranky because you're hungry," he said patiently. He gallantly pulled a chair out and gestured for her to sit. "But we'll fix that."

Elizabeth sat down, and Bruce hurried over to the stove and took out a pan of sizzling hamburgers. Then he efficiently put the pan down on the counter and turned off the stove.

I can't believe this is Bruce Patman I'm watching, Elizabeth thought, shaking her head.

He grabbed a pot holder, removed the tops of the vegetable pans, and took a deep sniff. "Ahhhh. Fresh vegetables."

Bruce picked up a dinner plate and began to serve the food. "I know we didn't plan on spinach, but I read the section on leafy greens and it talked about how healthy it is. So I brought some from home. Do you like spinach?"

"No," Elizabeth said bluntly.

She didn't. She hated spinach.

Plop!

Bruce dropped a big green blob of it on her

plate. It was as if he hadn't even heard her. "Don't think of it as spinach. Think of it as a source of iron. According to the manual, women need to be especially careful to get enough iron in their diet."

He put a hamburger, some squash, and some rice on her plate. Then he brought it to the table. "Here you go," he said. "Doesn't that look good?"

Elizabeth stared down angrily at her plate as Bruce fixed his own. He was treating her like a child, and she knew she was acting like one, but that blob of spinach was the biggest, greenest, smelliest blob of spinach in the whole world.

"Nutrition is so important," he babbled happily, ignoring her sulky face. "I think a husband and father should know a lot about nutrition."

"Uh huh," Elizabeth responded irritably.

Bruce smiled. "I've really worked hard on this Mr. Family-Man stuff. And you know what? I think I'm getting pretty good at it."

He suddenly looked a little embarrassed. "Listen, don't tell any of my friends about this, OK? I don't think they understand the full importance of family yet, the way I do."

Elizabeth wondered if she was going to be sick.

The door opened and Mr. Seigel came in. "Smells good," he said.

"It is good," Bruce said. "Isn't it, Elizabeth?"

"Sure," Elizabeth answered, frowning at her spinach.

Mr. Seigel looked at the table and nodded approvingly. "Very good. Very good. Well-balanced meal. Thoughtful presentation. Nicely set table. Excellent. Excellent."

"Would you like to join us?" Bruce asked politely. "We have plenty."

Mr. Seigel gave Bruce an odd look. "Thank you, but I don't believe I will. I'm not fond of spinach."

"Don't think of it as food," Bruce said seriously. "Think of it as a source of iron."

"I try not to think of it at all," Mr. Seigel said dryly. "Carry on. Finish your meal. I'll be back later to check your cleanup."

Mr. Seigel gave them a wave and hurried out.

Bruce shook his head regretfully. "I'm going to make a copy of that article on spinach for Mr. Seigel. Maybe he doesn't know how hard it is to get enough iron. You know what else? The manual said most people don't get enough calcium, either."

He chewed thoughtfully and swallowed. "Come to think of it, Elizabeth, I haven't seen you drink any milk lately. But don't worry. I'm going to start reminding you to drink some every day at lunch."

Elizabeth raised her eyes and stared across

the table in horror. What had Bruce turned into? Given the choice between Mr. Cool and Mr. Family Man, she'd take Mr. Cool any day. At least Mr. Cool didn't make a career out of telling her what to eat.

"Gee, thanks," she said sarcastically. "What would I do without you?"

Bruce smiled and nodded. "No problem. That's what husbands are for. Now don't forget to eat that spinach."

That did it.

Before she even knew what she was doing, Elizabeth picked up her plate and threw it on the floor. "I told you!" she shouted. "I hate spinach! Why don't you listen to anything I say?"

Bruce's mouth fell open and a piece of squash fell out. He blinked several times. Then he calmly put the piece of squash back in his mouth.

"You know," he said conversationally, "I'll bet you don't get enough sleep. I read in the manual about people who don't get enough sleep."

I'm never getting married, Elizabeth thought, gritting her teeth. *Never, never, never.*

Nine

◇

"How about spaghetti?" Patrick suggested.

Sophia sighed. It was their third trip to the grocery store, and they were making no progress at all. By now it was Thursday, and Mr. Seigel had rescheduled their kitchen time twice. Finally he'd told them not to sign up for any more time until they were absolutely certain that they were ready to make their meal.

The last possible time was tomorrow afternoon. If they didn't get their act together today, they were going to blow it.

They'd discussed making hamburgers, tuna casserole, baked fish, fried chicken, meat loaf, and tofu. Now they were right back where they had started—with spaghetti.

"Fine," Sophia snapped. She snatched a box of spaghetti noodles off the shelf and threw it in the cart.

"We don't have to make spaghetti if you don't want to," Patrick said quickly.

"Spaghetti is fine," Sophia said abruptly.

Patrick frowned in bewilderment. "Then why do you look so mad?"

"I'm just getting tired of waiting for you to make a decision," she finally exploded. "We're running out of time. We still haven't even signed up for kitchen time and tomorrow's the last day available."

Patrick's face darkened. "Well, I'm getting tired of waiting for *you* to make a decision."

"Then why can't you just speak up and say what's on your mind? Why do you always have to be so polite? It's getting on my nerves."

"I haven't noticed you speaking up, either," Patrick said in a defiant voice.

"That's because *you* never speak up."

Patrick folded his arms over his chest and jutted his jaw stubbornly. "Well, if you think I'm too polite, I'll be happy to stop."

"Good," Sophia said through gritted teeth. "Now what do you want to make?"

Patrick's eyes narrowed angrily. "Whatever you want to make is fine with me," he responded in a tight voice.

Sophia stamped her foot angrily. "What's the matter with you? You're impossible!"

"You're the one who's impossible!" Patrick shouted. "I'm just trying to be nice and cooperative. And let me tell you something: It's not easy being nice and cooperative with somebody as indecisive as you."

"I am not indecisive," Sophia snapped. "I'm the most decisive person I know."

"Then make a decision," Patrick challenged.

"How can I make a decision if you won't tell me what you want to make!"

"I told you what I want to make. I want to make whatever you want to make."

Sophia felt like she might really explode. Patrick Morris wasn't a nice guy. He was a wimp. A big, dumb, indecisive, overly polite wimp.

"I've had it with you . . . you . . . you big wimp!" she yelled.

"I've had it with you, too!" Patrick yelled back. "You sure are turning out to be different than I thought you were. I thought you were smart and outspoken, but you're not. You're too chicken even to say what's on your mind!"

"Who are you calling chicken?" Sophia shouted.

"Who are you calling wimp?" Patrick bellowed back.

Then he turned around and stalked out of the grocery store.

* * *

"Can't you do anything yourself?" Jessica fumed on Thursday afternoon as she and Rick struggled with the meal they were trying to make in the home-economics kitchen. She hurried over to the burning pot and grabbed the top. "OUCH!" she shouted, pulling her scalded hand away.

"Real smart, airhead. Try using a pot holder next time."

Jessica ran to the sink and held her hand under some cold water.

For the first time in her life, she understood what it must be like to be Elizabeth.

Jessica knew she tended to be a bit irresponsible. Maybe it was because she was used to having her responsible sister to depend on.

But Rick Hunter was much more irresponsible than she ever was. And since *somebody* had to be responsible, Jessica was forced to do it.

As soon as the sting faded a little, she hurried back to the pot and lifted the top with a pot holder.

"Look at this mess," she wailed. Every ounce of water had boiled away, and the noodles were burned and stuck to the bottom of the pot. "You were supposed to take these off the burner when they were done."

"Hey," Rick said with a shrug, "it's not my

fault. You should have reminded me to set the timer."

Jessica grabbed the pot and scraped the noodles into the garbage. "You're such a bonehead, Rick!"

Just then, something acrid in the air made her nose itch. It seemed to be making Rick's nose itch, too, because he sniffed and looked around.

Jessica and Rick both saw the smoke at the same time.

"FIRE!" Rick yelled dramatically.

Black smoke was seeping out of the oven.

"The bread!" Jessica shouted. "Get the bread!"

Rick ran to the oven and pulled open the door. A blast of heat nearly knocked him over. "Good grief!" he choked, fishing the burned black bread out of the back of the stove. "You were supposed to heat it, not incinerate it, airhead."

"*You* were supposed to heat it, *bonehead*!" Jessica snapped. "But you forgot, so I had to do it—along with everything else. No wonder I put it on the wrong temperature."

"Cooking's just not my thing," Rick said with a casual laugh. "Looks like it's not yours, either."

Jessica was too angry to speak.

Rick brought the bread over to the garbage can and threw it in on top of the ruined noodles.

"Let's eat out," he suggested. "What do you say?"

Jessica glared at him for a moment, then shoved the pot she was holding in his direction. "I say wash this."

Rick saluted. "Yes *sir!*" He took the pot over to the sink and quickly washed it. Then he dried it with a paper towel and put it on his head like a helmet.

"Any further orders, *sir?*" he shouted like a Marine.

Jessica grabbed the eggs from the refrigerator so she could start making the egg custard. "Quit fooling around," she ordered. "We're already way behind schedule. Mr. Seigel's going to be in here any minute."

Rick took two big kitchen spoons and began to bang a drum roll on the pot on his head. "And now, the man you've all been waiting for . . . MR. SEIGEL!"

Rick tapped the top of the oven with the spoon so that it sounded like a cymbal.

Then he snatched the pot from his head and pretended to be Mr. Seigel. "Hmmmm," he muttered in a deep voice. He peered into the empty pot. "What is this nutritious dish?"

He stepped to the side and pretended to flip his hair like Jessica. "It's earthworm stew," he said in a high voice.

In spite of the fact that she was ready to kill

Rick, Jessica smiled. It was a pretty good imitation of her. Even though he was teasing her, she felt kind of flattered to know that he watched her that closely.

"Earthworm stew!" Rick exclaimed in his Mr. Seigel voice. "My favorite. Is it a mix? Or did you make it from scratch?"

Rick switched his voice again and pretended to be Jessica. "Oh, we made it from scratch. We scratched around in the yard until we found the worms."

"Stop it," Jessica said, trying not to laugh.

But Rick was having too much fun. He pretended to rub the bridge of his nose, just like Mr. Seigel did when he was about to ask a question. "And what's for dessert?"

"Well," Rick said, imitating Jessica's breathiest tones, "actually, we have these delicious brownies made from nutritious Doggie De-Lite dog food. It's my own recipe."

Rick licked his lips and cleared his throat like Mr. Seigel. "I hope you have enough for three. Doggie De-Lite brownies are my favorite."

Jessica couldn't help it. She was laughing so hard she thought her sides would split. "You sound just like Mr. Seigel," she choked out. "He looks like the dog-food type, doesn't he?"

Rick threw back his head and laughed.

"Actually," a voice said behind them, "I prefer ice cream with blueberries."

Jessica's laughter came to an abrupt halt and she felt her heart thud.

Mr. Seigel was standing in the doorway, looking at them disapprovingly.

Jessica's throat tightened. He'd probably seen and heard the whole thing. She tried to remember what she'd said. *He looks like the dog-food type, doesn't he?* She felt like crying. Mr. Seigel had a pretty good sense of humor sometimes, but he didn't look amused at all as he surveyed the kitchen.

He stepped over and examined the ruined food in the garbage can. "Wasteful and unnecessary," he commented.

Jessica and Rick stood there staring at him in embarrassed silence.

"You two have been in here an hour," he said sharply. "You should have been finished by now. I suggest you stop being silly and get to work."

"Yes, sir," Jessica said softly, turning back to her work.

"Yes, sir," Rick echoed, hurrying to fill the pot with water.

"I'm giving you twenty more minutes. When I get back, I expect to see the table set, the food prepared, and the two of you sitting down like civilized adults. I don't care who does what. What's important is that you somehow accomplish the task assigned—together. Understand?"

Jessica nodded, watching Mr. Seigel's angry face.

"Then *move*," he practically shouted. He left the room and shut the door behind him with a bang.

Rick and Jessica both sprang into action. Rick quickly filled the spaghetti pot with more water, and Jessica turned back to her egg custard. Her hand reached automatically toward the egg carton, and one by one, she began cracking eggs into the mixing bowl.

She could feel her cheeks flushing hot with embarrassment. She and Rick were probably the most inept couple in the whole school. They'd probably get the worst grade anybody ever received in the whole history of the school.

Jessica's mind was working so fast, she didn't hear Rick yell, "STOP!" until it was too late.

Jessica smacked the last egg onto the edge of the bowl, wishing she were cracking it over Rick Hunter's pointy head.

CRACKKK!!

Jessica closed her hand angrily over the shell, crushing it between her fingers.

"Uh oh," she heard Rick say.

Jessica looked down and her eyes widened in horror. "No," she whispered.

"I tried to tell you," Rick began.

"Oh, no," she said again.

"The egg carton seemed like a good place to put him," Rick said.

"Please say you didn't," Jessica squeaked. She slowly opened her fist and looked down. In her palm was a pile of crushed eggshell. And in the middle of the pile was a little blue sticker.

Rick began to laugh.

Jessica felt her face turning red with rage. How dare he laugh? How *dare* he?

Jessica closed her eyes and balled her fists. "I don't understand it!" she screamed at the top of her lungs. "You're ruining this project! You're ruining my clothes! *And you're ruining my life!* If you hate me so much, just say so, *instead of making my life—*"

But Jessica never got to finish her sentence, because the next thing she knew, Rick leaned forward and kissed her lightly, right on the mouth.

Jessica's eyes flew open in shock.

Rick stepped back suddenly, looking just as shocked and surprised.

They stared at each other for a moment. Then Rick began to smile shyly. Jessica's heart skipped a beat.

Ten

◇

Sophia sat on a bench outside the grocery store, staring glumly into space. Tears of frustration and confusion welled up in her eyes. She knew she should go home. But she was too miserable to move.

She'd finally said what was on her mind. And Patrick had said what was on *his* mind. And look what happened!

Marriage was a no-win situation, she decided. If you respected each other's thoughts and feelings, you were miserable. And if you spoke up and said what was on your mind, it started a fight. She and Patrick had been a great couple. They really and truly liked each other. If they couldn't make it work, nobody could.

And as awful as it was, she still liked Patrick. Even after all the rotten things they had said to each other. In fact, she liked him *better* now that she knew he wasn't too wimpy to say what he really thought.

But now Patrick didn't like her.

What a mess.

Marriage stinks, she told herself angrily. *I can't believe I actually fell for this idiotic romance stuff. Just look what a big wimp it's turned* me *into.*

"Sophia!" Sophia's brother, Tony, stood at the front door of the Rizzo home, waving at her. "We thought you'd never get here."

"What's up?" she asked dully. Not that she cared. She was too miserable to get excited about anything right now. She was exhausted, too. She'd walked all the way home instead of taking the bus. She'd needed some time to think.

Tony grabbed her by the sleeve and tugged her inside the house. "Come on. Come in the kitchen."

Sophia followed Tony down the hall. From inside the kitchen, she could hear the sound of her mother's laughter.

When she stepped into the kitchen, she saw Mr. Thomas sitting at the table with his daughter, Sarah, and Sophia's mother. They all broke into broad smiles when they saw Sophia.

"We've been waiting for you," Mrs. Rizzo said excitedly. "Sit. Sit."

Sophia sat down and looked around the table at their beaming faces. "What's up? What are you all so happy about?"

Mr. Thomas handed Sophia a glass of lemonade and poured one for Tony. Then he cleared his throat and stood. "Now that we're all here, I have an announcement to make."

Sarah's eyes caught Sophia's and she smiled.

What is going on here? Sophia wondered.

Mr. Thomas lifted his glass. "As of two o'clock this afternoon, Maria and I are engaged to be married. The wedding will be held two weeks from this Sunday, and you are all invited."

Tony and Sarah began to shout and applaud. But Sophia felt her heart sinking right down into her shoes.

"Isn't it great?" Tony crowed. He nudged Sophia's arm.

Every pair of eyes at the table turned toward Sophia. And on each face, Sophia saw happiness and enthusiasm.

She tried to force the lines of her face into a smile, but she couldn't. She just couldn't do it. In spite of all her efforts, her mouth began to turn down and her brows began to furrow.

Mr. Thomas put his arm around Sophia's

mother and hugged her. "What do you think, Sophia? Think we'll make a good couple?"

Sophia didn't answer.

"Sophia?" Mrs. Rizzo said, her smile beginning to waver. "Is something wrong?"

Sarah's face began to grow concerned, and so did Tony's. "Say something, Soph," Tony urged.

Patrick's voice still echoed in the back of her mind. *You're too chicken to say what you really think.* Well, she wasn't. Not anymore.

Sophia stood angrily and slammed her glass of lemonade down on the table. "Marriage stinks!" she shouted.

"Sophia!" her mother said sharply.

"It does. And I think you're making a big mistake."

"Shut up, Sophia," Tony said angrily. "You're spoiling everything."

"*Marriage* spoils everything," Sophia insisted tearfully. "It makes people act like pathetic wimps. I'm never getting married."

She stumbled out of the kitchen and ran blindly down the hall to her room. She slammed the door shut and locked it. Then she threw herself facedown on the bed and began to sob.

Elizabeth lay on her bed staring grumpily at the wall. She knew she should be working on her summary notes for the marriage project. But what was the use? Bruce was probably going to write the whole summary himself.

As far as Elizabeth was concerned, she never wanted to hear the word "marriage" again. The whole thing had been a total fiasco.

She felt the blood rush to her face as she remembered throwing her plate of spinach on the floor. How could she have stooped so low? And even that hadn't gotten Bruce's attention. There was no question about it, marriage was turning them all into lunatics.

At that moment the door to her bedroom flew open and Jessica came rushing in. "Guess what," Jessica proclaimed, pulling up short at her bed.

"You filed for divorce," Elizabeth offered gloomily.

"Nope," Jessica said. "Not even close." She looked around excitedly. "It's so amazing. You better be sitting down for this, Lizzie."

"Jessica, I'm *lying* down. Tell me already."

Jessica took a deep breath. "I may be getting an *F* from Mr. Seigel, but I just had the most romantic meal of my entire life."

"Are you kidding? With who?"

"Rick Hunter."

Elizabeth stared at her in amazement. "What are you talking about?" she demanded. "You and Rick, romantic? You two make Bruce and me look like Romeo and Juliet."

Jessica laughed. "I know we fought a lot, but I think I finally understand why," she said. "You see, the whole time, Rick and I actually had crushes on each other. He teased me so much because he *liked* me."

Elizabeth shook her head and flopped back on her pillows. "Jess, I give up. This whole marriage thing is totally beyond me. Wake me when it's over."

"How's your pizza?" Rick asked Jessica politely. They were sitting together in the cafeteria on Friday at lunch.

"Fine," Jessica said. "How's your macaroni and cheese?"

"Fine," Rick responded. "I think it's my very favorite food now."

Jessica swallowed. "Really?"

"Yeah."

"Oh."

In the awkward silence Jessica could hear lots of couples bickering around them.

"Can you believe Mr. Seigel made us eat that whole meal yesterday?" Jessica asked.

Rick shook his head. "Uh uh. And I can't believe I put molasses on the salad instead of olive oil."

Jessica laughed. "I still can't figure out how I managed to put mustard in the egg custard. It was the most disgusting thing I've ever eaten."

Rick laughed. "Not for me. I thought it was great." He cleared his throat and looked at her with a serious expression. "I guess because you made it."

Jessica opened her mouth, but she couldn't think of anything to say. So she just blushed and looked down at her plate.

Silence.

Jessica waited nervously, hoping Rick would say something funny, but he just stared down at his plate, too.

"So . . . um . . ." Jessica began finally. "Do you think Mr. Seigel will, uh, pass us?"

"Yeah, I hope so," Rick answered. "Unless he gets really technical over the eggs."

Jessica began to blush again. Lots of couples had broken their eggs or lost them—but none of them had managed to break as many as Jessica.

"Not that it was your fault," Rick said quickly, noticing Jessica's embarrassed face. "What I mean is, most of the time, it was really *my* fault."

Jessica smiled.

Then Rick smiled.

Silence.

We sure had more to talk about when we were enemies, Jessica couldn't help thinking.

She racked her brain for something to say, but she couldn't think of anything. So she smiled again, hoping Rick would say something.

But he didn't. He just cleared his throat. Then he took another bite of his macaroni and cheese.

Oh, well, Jessica thought. *When you have romance, who needs conversation?*

Eleven

◇

"OK," the waiter said. "Who had the butterscotch sundae?"

"I did," Ellen Riteman answered quickly. "So anyway. I told Winston—"

"And who had the two scoops of cookies-and-cream with rainbow sprinkles?" the waiter asked, interrupting Ellen.

"I did," Tamara Chase said.

It was Saturday afternoon, and the Unicorns were gathered at Casey's, the ice-cream parlor at the Valley Mall. They had a lot of catching up to do, since they hadn't been able to eat at the Uni-corner, their regular lunch table, in two weeks. They were all so busy talking, they weren't paying any attention to the waiter or each other.

As the waiter passed the ice cream around, Jessica waited for her friends to notice that she hadn't ordered anything. She couldn't wait for somebody to ask her *why* she hadn't ordered anything. Because the answer was that Rick was coming to meet her for ice cream at Casey's later that afternoon.

She knew they were all going to be green with envy when they heard about her big romance. She knew they'd want to know every detail.

Jessica clinked her spoon on the table a few times and took a loud sip of her water, but nobody seemed to notice that she hadn't ordered any ice cream.

"Randy and I are probably going to get an *F*," Janet was saying irritably. "And it's all Randy's fault. You should have seen him in the kitchen. He acts like it's some kind of a science experiment. He measures *everything*—in grams! Our meal was a disaster."

"That's nothing. You should try cooking with Winston," Ellen said. "He's allergic to everything. Chicken gives him hives. Beef gives him headaches. Dairy products give him a stomachache. We finally ended up making rice for dinner. Rice."

"Will you please shut up about Winston Egbert's allergies?" Janet demanded. "I'm sick of hearing you whine and complain. Anyway, did I tell you what Randy did to the noodles?"

"Speaking of noodles," Jessica said, giggling, "the funniest thing happened when Rick and I made our—"

"You should have seen Todd washing the dishes," Lila interrupted. "He's a neatness freak. He rinsed each fork for about twenty minutes. I missed *Days of Turmoil* yesterday because of Todd and his dumb forks." She gave a huffy sigh. "We haven't turned in our budget yet, and you know why? Because he hasn't found a folder that looks neat enough. Can you believe that? Like it really matters."

"Well, you are a little sloppy sometimes," Tamara said.

"Sloppy! Me?"

"Yeah. Remember that time Ms. Luster told you your book report was unreadable because it was covered with peanut butter?"

"It was not peanut butter," Lila said indignantly. "It was paté."

"Lots of people haven't turned in their budgets," Tamara said dolefully.

"Rick and I argued a lot about our budget," Jessica began. "But then I—"

"Lots of people never made their meal," Belinda Layton put in. "Dennis Cookman and I never even got any kitchen time because Denny and Cammi took so long. And Mr. Seigel wouldn't do anything about it."

"Rick does a really funny imitation of Mr. Seigel," Jessica said eagerly. "He—"

"I knew that marriage was going to be a disaster," Janet Howell interrupted loudly. "Denny is way too good for Cammi. She never has two words to say for herself. And her clothes are seriously ugly."

"I heard that they lost their egg," Mandy Miller said.

"Figures," Janet said.

"Lots of people lost their eggs," Mary Wallace added with a sigh.

"Lots of people are going to fail," Belinda predicted darkly.

"Thank goodness it's over Monday," Betsy Gordon said. "One more study hall. That's it."

"Yeah," Tamara said. "But it's going to be a killer study hall. Two hours."

Mandy nodded. "Mr. Seigel said each couple has to prepare a written summary of their experience and finish their budgets if they haven't turned them in. They have to return their eggs and submit a detailed account of who did what with the egg and when—"

"And we all have to turn in a meal plan for two weeks," Mary Wallace added. "And the worst part is—"

"We know," Lila said.

"It has to be completed as a couple," they all said in unison.

Tamara shrugged in confusion. "It all sounded so romantic at first. What happened?"

"Romantic! How can marriage be romantic when you're married to somebody like Randy Mason?" Janet groaned.

Suddenly, everybody was talking at once again.

But it is romantic! Jessica thought sullenly. *It really is.*

"So. Are you going to have some ice cream?" Rick asked as Jessica slid into a booth across from him later that afternoon.

"Sure," Jessica said.

He smiled at her and Jessica waited for him to say something about how ice cream was going to ruin her modeling career. Now that she knew he teased her because he liked her, she didn't mind at all. She'd just get him with a snappy comeback and they'd both laugh.

Rick smiled.

Jessica waited.

He opened his mouth.

Jessica started thinking up her comeback.

"What kind of ice cream do you want?" he asked politely.

Jessica's face fell. "Uh . . . chocolate," she said.

Silence.

"So, uh, Monday's the end of the project," Jessica said, trying to sound perky.

"Yep."

"I sure hope Mr. Seigel doesn't flunk me. My parents would kill me," she said.

"I hope he doesn't flunk you, either," Rick said agreeably.

"And I hope he doesn't flunk *you*," Jessica added quickly.

"Thanks."

Silence.

Geez, Jessica thought. *Being romantic sure is exhausting.*

"Jessica!" Mrs. Wakefield shouted from the kitchen on Sunday night. "It's Rick Hunter."

Jessica ran out of her room and grabbed the telephone in the upstairs hall. "Hello," she said eagerly.

"What are you doing?" Rick asked.

"Not much," Jessica replied. "Just getting all my notes ready for the study hall tomorrow. What are you doing?"

There was a long pause.

Then Rick sighed soulfully. "Thinking of you."

Jessica's eyes widened.

It was a romantic thing to say. But it wasn't

like Rick at all. In fact, it was kind of . . . *embarrassing*.

She swallowed. She had no idea what to say.

She had thought it was so great that Rick wasn't making fun of her anymore—that he had gone from being obnoxious to being nice.

But she was actually beginning to miss the old Rick.

"It'll never last," Sophia insisted.

Her mother shook her head in confusion. "Why do you keep saying that? Why shouldn't it last? I thought you liked Mr. Thomas."

"Do you like Mr. Thomas?" Sophia asked.

"Well, of course I do."

"Then that's why it'll never work."

Mrs. Rizzo threw up her hands. "Why do you keep saying that? Of course it'll work."

Sophia and her mother were standing in the kitchen on Sunday evening, cleaning up after dinner.

"I think you have some kind of flu," Mrs. Rizzo said finally. "That's why you are being so sad and morbid."

"I don't have the flu, Mama. I'm just upset because I think you're making a huge mistake."

"I just don't understand where you are getting all these silly ideas. Why shouldn't our marriage work? I love Mr. Thomas and he loves me."

"It doesn't matter how much you love each

other," Sophia argued. "Oh, sure. Things start out romantic. But if you want to keep things romantic, you can't really be yourself. You're so busy respecting each other's thoughts and feelings that you never say what you really think or how you really feel." Sophia's voice rose in frustration. "But eventually, you *have* to be yourself. And he has to be *himself*. And then you wind up shouting at each other in the grocery store—*with a whole bunch of people staring at you like you are some kind of lunatic!*" she finished with a shout.

Mrs. Rizzo stared at her daughter in bewilderment. "What in the world are you talking about?"

"I'm talking about marriage. Take it from me, Mama, it's a bad idea. I should know. I've been married for two whole weeks."

Twelve

◇

The atmosphere in the cafeteria was tense. All around Jessica and Rick, couples were feverishly trying to finish up their projects.

"Time's almost up," Mr. Seigel warned. "I want all written sections handed in by the end of this study hall."

"You've added those numbers five times," Jessica heard Todd hiss at Lila. "And you've gotten five different answers."

"You do it if you think you're so smart," Lila hissed back.

"I'm getting the folder ready. Besides, how smart do you have to be to add?" Todd asked sarcastically.

"Would you quit bugging me?" Lila

snapped. "We're running out of time. Help me finish this and quit fooling around with that folder."

Rick smiled at Jessica. "That's what we used to sound like. I'm glad we don't sound like that anymore."

Jessica nodded. "Me, too." *I guess*, she added to herself.

"I don't ever want to fight with you again, Jessica."

Jessica searched his face carefully for signs of sarcasm. But he wasn't being sarcastic at all. He was totally serious.

"You're way too nice to fight with," he added sincerely.

Jessica chewed nervously on her thumbnail. Maybe that would get him to snap out of it. It was exactly the kind of thing he used to tease her about.

But Rick just gave her a misty smile. "You look so cute when you chew your nail like that."

Gag! she thought. "OK," she said briskly, trying to change the subject. "Let's try to get this report finished." She flipped through her papers. "We blew the child-care section. And the meal preparation. But fortunately, we do have a good budget."

"Thanks to you." Rick smiled.

Jessica couldn't help preening. "I did do a good job on the budget, didn't I?"

Rick nodded.

"And I did it all by myself, too."

Rick frowned. "I know."

"I guess I didn't need you to help after all."

Rick's eyes narrowed. "I guess not."

She giggled. "I don't know why I thought you'd be any help with it. You're even worse in math than I am. I guess I did wind up learning a lot from this marriage project. I learned that I can do a lot more things than I thought I could. And I can do them by myself."

"All right!" he snapped. "I get the point!"

Jessica blinked in surprise. "What are you getting so mad about?"

"I'm not mad," Rick said. "But I guess I learned a couple of things too—like it's stupid to be nice to a girl if all she's going to do is put me down for not doing some dumb budget."

"I'm not putting you down," Jessica protested.

"Yes, you are. I'm getting sick of listening to you brag about that budget and tell me what an idiot I am."

Jessica narrowed her eyes. "You just don't want to hear about it because *I* did it and *you* didn't."

"Would you guys keep it down?" Dennis Cookman said irritably from the other end of the table. "You're distracting us."

Jessica whirled angrily in Dennis Cookman's

direction. But before she could say a word, she heard Janet Howell's voice rising behind her.

"Thanks to you this whole project has been a disaster!" she shouted at Randy.

"Thanks to *me*!" Randy retorted. "I'm not the one who's impossible to get along with. If you had just listened to me when I explained to you—"

"Why should I listen to you? What do you know about anything? You haven't learned one thing from this."

"I learned that I'm glad I'm not *really* married to you!" Randy shouted.

At the other end of the table, Elizabeth jumped. She couldn't believe it. Randy was usually so quiet.

She looked over at Bruce to see how he was reacting to all the tension that was brewing in the cafeteria. But Bruce was placidly writing their child-care summary. He seemed happily oblivious to everything going on around him.

"Now," he said, "I think we're in good shape. We've completed every section of the project." His pencil moved across the page. "And our summary is turning out very nicely," he added proudly.

"Don't you think you should at least let me look at the summary?" Elizabeth asked irritably.

"After all, it's supposed to reflect *both* of our experiences."

Bruce laughed lightly. "I think you know by now that you can trust me to do a good job." He looked up and smiled at Elizabeth. "You know what I'm the proudest of?"

He tapped the little egg carrier sitting at his elbow. "I'm really proud that we haven't lost or broken our egg. I think we're one of the few couples who can say that."

Elizabeth swallowed hard. "Uh huh," she whispered.

"Okay, folks, five more minutes," Mr. Seigel called out.

Elizabeth tapped her fingers on the table impatiently as Bruce read over their summary.

"I do *not* chew with my mouth open!" Elizabeth heard someone bellow at the top of his voice.

She and Bruce both jumped in surprise, and his elbow tapped the carrier.

"Look out!" Elizabeth shouted.

Bruce quickly tried to steady it, but it was too late. The carrier tipped off the table and the egg fell to the floor.

THUMP!

Bruce stared down at the floor, his face frozen. "It didn't break," he whispered hoarsely.

"It didn't?" Elizabeth breathed.

Bruce shook his head and looked confused. "*Why* didn't it break?"

Elizabeth shook her head in bewilderment.

Bruce leaned over and retrieved the egg from the floor. He held it up, and they both peered at it.

A tiny network of spidery lines covered one side of it.

Very carefully, Bruce reached over and pulled the tiniest bit of shell from the egg.

Then, he smacked the egg down on the table. "*It's hard-boiled!*" he bellowed. "Someone pulled a switcheroo!" He turned and glared at Elizabeth. "And that someone was you!"

Elizabeth shook her head in confusion. "I don't understand . . ."

"Thanks a whole bunch, Elizabeth! You didn't trust me not to break the egg, so you gave me a hard-boiled one. The manual said couples were supposed to trust each other."

"The manual also said couples were supposed to listen to each other," Elizabeth shot back. She was so angry that her hands were shaking. "You know what your problem is, Bruce? You don't *listen.* Mr. Cool didn't listen, and Mr. Family Man doesn't, either."

"That does it!" Bruce shouted. He began to tear up the summary into little pieces. "What's the point of giving something my best shot if nobody appreciates it? I'm never getting married. *Never!"*

Bruce's voice seemed to be the signal everyone had been waiting for.

"Me neither!" Rick Hunter shouted, jumping to his feet.

"I'm never getting married, either," Lila Fowler yelled.

"Quiet!" Mr. Seigel shouted. "Quiet! Quiet! Finish the project!"

"I don't need to finish the project," Patrick Morris yelled. "Because I'm never getting married!"

"Neither am I," Sophia yelled back.

Janet Howell threw her manual at Randy. "I'm not finishing this project. I don't care what grade I get."

Mr. Seigel clapped his hands again. "QUIET! QUIET!" he warned.

But it was no use. The cafeteria was totally out of control.

Across the cafeteria, Aaron and Veronica were playing tug of war with their report. "Give me that!" Aaron demanded.

"OK. Take it!" Veronica exclaimed, suddenly letting go. There was a surprised shout as Aaron tumbled backward in his seat.

An egg came flying across the cafeteria. Elizabeth ducked just as it whizzed over her head and smacked Todd Wilkins on the back.

"Hey!" Todd yelled in protest.

"I don't want to hear one more word about my handwriting!" Elizabeth heard Lloyd Benson shouting from across the room. "You can write up the stupid summary if you want!"

"I refuse to do one more thing on this project!" came an even louder voice.

"This project is impossible!"

The whole cafeteria burst into applause and shouts of agreement.

"What did you say?" Mr. Seigel asked with an innocent smile.

"It's impossible!" a bunch of people shouted.

Mr. Seigel lifted his eyebrows in surprise. "It is? Tell me why. In a *normal* tone of voice, *please*!" He looked out over the cafeteria. "It is not necessary to shout in order to be heard."

Randy Mason raised his hand. "Look, Mr. Seigel, you can't just pick people's names out of a hat, tell them they're married, and then expect them to work well together. It's rigged. We're all going to fail."

Mr. Seigel rubbed his chin thoughtfully. "Don't *any* of you think you were successful with this project?"

The cafeteria was silent.

"You mean you all think you have failed?"

Several heads nodded.

He looked at them for another moment of silence.

"Then you have learned more than you think. You haven't failed. You may tear up your reports. The point has been made. You will each receive an *A*."

"What?" Todd shouted.

Mr. Seigel's face grew serious. "You have all just had one small taste of what you are up against if you rush into marriage without thinking it through. Think how hard these last two weeks have been. Would you want to spend a lifetime being that unhappy?"

Mr. Seigel sat down on the edge of one of the tables. "What I've been trying to demonstrate to you is that when you marry someone you don't know very well, and with whom you have not discussed the responsibilities and roles involved, you might as well marry someone . . . well . . ." He grinned at the students. ". . . whose name you picked out of a hat."

There was a stunned silence in the cafeteria. Then the room erupted into talking and laughter.

"You mean we don't have to finish the budgets?" Sophia asked.

"No."

"We don't have to worry about these stupid eggs anymore?" Ellen Riteman demanded.

"No."

"We don't have to do *anything*?" Denny Jacobson asked with a disbelieving smile.

"Well, I wouldn't go that far," Mr. Seigel responded with a laugh. "You're only in middle school. You've got a lot of things to do over the next several years. You've got high school to finish. College to attend. Careers to start. However, getting married and raising children can wait. You're only young once. So enjoy it while you can."

Janet Howell smiled. "I knew the whole thing was a joke."

"This project was not a joke," Mr. Seigel corrected. "It was a serious project designed to make you think carefully about what marriage and children really mean."

"But Mr. Seigel, are you saying marriage doesn't work?" Brooke Dennis asked.

"Of course not. When a marriage works, it's wonderful. But both partners have to be clear about what they expect to get out of the marriage, and what they are willing to put into it. Sure, marriage is romantic. But it takes hard work to keep it that way. Because the real romance is in spending your life with someone you respect and trust. Someone whose expectations are as realistic as your own."

Every student in the cafeteria was quiet and thoughtful.

"That is all," Mr. Seigel finally said. "You are dismissed."

Thirteen

◇

Sophia sat quietly in the back of the cafeteria. As she had listened to Mr. Seigel, she'd felt tears welling up in her eyes. But the heavy lump that she'd been carrying around in her stomach was finally beginning to dissolve.

She realized now that she had been all wrong about her mother and Mr. Thomas. They were perfect for each other.

Just because she and Patrick weren't ready to get married, that didn't mean her mom and Mr. Thomas weren't. Sophia and Patrick were only in sixth grade. Her mom and Mr. Thomas were grown up and responsible. They'd both been married before, too. It wasn't as if they didn't know what to expect.

She looked across the cafeteria and saw Sarah Thomas looking hopefully in her direction, trying to catch her eye.

Suddenly, Sophia's heart soared. Two weeks from Sunday, she'd have a father and a sister. As soon as she got home, she was going to tell her mother how she really felt, and apologize for being so gloomy.

At that moment she noticed Patrick across the table giving her a sheepish smile. Sophia smiled back.

"I'm sorry," she said softly, piling up her notebooks in front of her on the table. "I didn't mean to call you a wimp."

"*You* don't need to be sorry," he said quickly. "*I'm* the one who's sorry."

Sophia pursed her lips in irritation. Patrick caught the look and grinned.

"Uh oh. Let's not start this again." He laughed. "Okay, Sophia Rizzo, you *should* be sorry."

"Well, I said I was," Sophia began hotly. "You don't have to—"

"Hang on," Patrick said, holding up his hands. "I'm sorry, too." He laughed. "Now that we don't have to worry about this project anymore, can we go back to being friends? And will you go back to being the way you used to be? You know what I mean—outspoken, but not at the top of your lungs."

"Sure." Sophia smiled. "If you'll promise to say what you really think and not worry so much about what I'm thinking."

"It's a deal," Patrick said.

Sophia began to load her books into her backpack. Suddenly she looked up. "Listen," she said, "I haven't checked with my mom yet, but if it's OK with her, would you like to come to a wedding with me in a couple of weeks?"

"What do you mean you *broke* the egg?" Bruce asked. "By accident?"

Elizabeth nodded. "At my house, that day when you were throwing a conniption fit over the joys of fatherhood." She put her elbows on the cafeteria table. "I didn't want you to find out about it, so I grabbed another egg out of the refrigerator. I guess they were all hard-boiled. But I didn't know it."

"Why didn't you just tell me?"

"Because you were taking it so seriously. You kept calling the egg 'baby.' And the worst thing was, you were accusing me of being irresponsible." She gave him a wry smile. "I guess I didn't want to prove you right."

Bruce shook his head. "Everybody's always talking about how responsible you are—I guess I was just trying to prove that I could be responsible, too—you know, like your dad."

"Yeah! But my dad doesn't prove he's

responsible by treating my mom like she's an idiot."

"I guess I got a little carried away," Bruce admitted.

Elizabeth rolled her eyes. "I'll say."

Bruce took a comb from his pocket and ran it through his hair.

It looked as though Mr. Cool was back. *Thank goodness*, Elizabeth thought.

"So listen," Bruce said, trying hard to keep his voice casual. "This husband and fatherhood thing was cool and all, but I'm afraid it's time to go back to my bachelor ways."

"OK," Elizabeth said agreeably.

He studied her for a moment. "But, uh, even though we're not married anymore, remember what I said. OK?"

"About what?"

"Calcium and iron," he answered.

Jessica looked up from packing her backpack and saw Lila giving Todd a grudging smile.

"I'm sorry we didn't get to use your folder," Lila said. "You really did a nice job on the label."

Todd nodded. "Thanks. I did the lettering with a calligraphy pen."

"Maybe you can use the folder for another report," Lila suggested helpfully. "It would be a shame to let it go to waste."

Jessica had to smile. If Lila could get along

with Todd, she could certainly get along with Rick. Maybe it was time for them to make up, too. But when she turned to face Rick, he was gone.

She looked quickly around the cafeteria and caught a last glimpse of Rick's back as he stalked angrily out of the cafeteria.

Fine, Jessica thought angrily. *If you don't want to make up, I don't want to make up, either.*

The next afternoon, Jessica hurried to the cafeteria. Now that the marriage project was over, she was really looking forward to sitting with the other Unicorns at their usual table. She might not have a big romance to talk about, but at least when the other Unicorns talked about how horrible their husbands had been, Jessica could complain, too.

As Jessica entered the cafeteria, she saw Lila coming out of the line with her tray. "Hi," Jessica said. "I'll get my tray and be over in a minute."

Lila nodded, but Jessica noticed that she wasn't heading toward the Unicorner.

"Aren't you going to sit at the Unicorner?" Jessica asked.

"I actually told Todd I'd sit with him for a couple of minutes," Lila answered, looking a little sheepish.

"Are you kidding? The marriage project is over," Jessica protested.

Lila shrugged. "I know. But Todd's been telling me this hilarious story about his cousin, and he just got a letter—Never mind. I'll be over there in a minute."

"Fine, I'll be at the Unicorner," Jessica said, heading for the line. "There's no way I'm sitting with Rick Hunter if I don't have to," she muttered to no one in particular.

By the time Jessica got through the lunch line with her tray, Janet Howell, Ellen Riteman, and a couple of the other Unicorns had gathered at the Unicorner.

As Jessica sat down beside Ellen, she noticed, to her amazement, that Randy Mason was sitting next to Janet.

"The most important invention in the history of science was *not* the telephone," Randy was arguing. "It was the microscope."

"That's ridiculous," Janet said. "I never use microscopes. But I couldn't exist without a phone."

Even though they were arguing, Jessica realized, they didn't sound angry. They sounded as if they were having fun.

"Why is Randy Mason sitting at the Unicorner?" Jessica whispered to Ellen.

"I don't know. He was walking by and Janet waved to him to sit down," Ellen whispered back. Then she laughed. "I guess they're kind of addicted to arguing."

"But the marriage project is *over*," Jessica insisted, feeling completely bewildered.

Ellen smiled and waved at Winston Egbert, who was sitting at a nearby table with Sarah Thomas and Jerry McAllister. Winston stood up and started to walk over to them.

"Don't tell me after all that complaining you actually *like* Winston Egbert!" Jessica exclaimed.

Ellen blushed. "It's not like we're *friends* or anything," she said defensively. "He just likes to hang around me. Can I help that?" She pushed a chair back for Winston. "Before you try to steal my brownie, I'll just give you half," she said cheerfully as he sat down.

Jessica shook her head in disbelief. Ellen was willingly sharing her brownie with Winston Egbert? What was going on here?

"So how's Rick Hunter?" Mandy asked as she plunked her tray down across from Jessica.

"The marriage project is *over*!" Jessica snapped. "Why does everyone keep talking about it?"

"My," Mandy said. "Aren't *you* in a good mood."

Jessica looked down at her macaroni and cheese and sighed. She couldn't help thinking about the meal she and Rick had made. She wished she'd gotten meat loaf for lunch instead.

"Sorry, Mandy," Jessica said, pushing her

plate aside. "Anyway, I don't think Rick likes me anymore."

"Tsk tsk tsk," a voice said.

Jessica looked up and saw Rick pulling up a chair across the table.

"You sure do eat a lot of starchy food for somebody who wants to be a model," he said with a grin.

Mandy frowned at Rick. "The marriage project is over, Rick, so why don't you quit teasing Jessica? No wonder you guys don't get along."

But neither Jessica nor Rick was paying any attention. They were smiling at each other across the table.

"We don't get along because Rick's a bonehead," Jessica said happily.

"That's not true," Rick protested. "We don't get along because Jessica's an airhead."

They looked at each other again and burst out laughing.

"I'm just glad it's over," Elizabeth said to Maria Slater, Amy Sutton, and Julie Porter, unwrapping her ice-cream sandwich.

"I may never eat another egg as long as I live," Maria said.

"It's kind of strange, though," Amy said. "Everyone hated being married so much, but the weirdest couples ended up being friends."

"Hey, Elizabeth," Bruce Patman said, breezing by their lunch table.

Amy laughed. "See what I mean?"

"Speaking of friends," Maria said, glancing toward the back of the cafeteria. "Why does Cammi Adams always sit alone?"

"I don't know. I've invited her to sit with me a bunch of times," Elizabeth said. "But she usually doesn't want to."

"She seems really nice, and she's a great reporter for the *Sixers*," Julie said. "I guess she's just shy."

"I heard her and Denny's marriage project was a total disaster," Maria said. "For some reason she got really anxious if Denny ever called her at home or suggested they work on their report after school."

Elizabeth nodded. "I once asked her for her number to discuss a *Sixers* feature with her, and she got sort of nervous about it. She suddenly had to run off."

Amy shrugged. "It's almost like she's hiding a big secret or something."

What is Cammi Adams trying to hide? Find out in Sweet Valley Twins No. 69, WON'T SOMEONE HELP ANNA?

We hope you enjoyed reading this book. If you would like to receive further information about available titles in the Bantam series, just write to the address below, with your name and address: Kim Prior, Bantam Books, 61–63 Uxbridge Road, Ealing, London W5 5SA.

If you live in Australia or New Zealand and would like more information about the series, please write to:

Sally Porter
Transworld Publishers
(Australia) Pty Ltd
15–25 Helles Avenue
Moorebank
NSW 2170
AUSTRALIA

Kiri Martin
Transworld Publishers (NZ) Ltd
3 William Pickering Drive
Albany
Auckland
NEW ZEALAND

All Bantam and Young Adult books are available at your bookshop or newsagent, or can be ordered from the following address: Corgi/Bantam Books, Cash Sales Department, PO Box 11, Falmouth, Cornwall, TR10 9EN.

Please list the title(s) you would like, and send together with a cheque or postal order to cover the cost of the book(s) plus postage and packing charges of £1.00 for one book, £1.50 for two books, and an additional 30p for each subsequent book ordered to a maximum of £3.00 for seven or more books.

(The above applies only to readers in the UK, and BFPO)

Overseas customers (including Eire), please allow £2.00 for postage and packing for the first book, an additional £1.00 for a second book, and 50p for each subsequent title ordered.

SWEET VALLEY TWINS

Don't miss the extra-long special editions of this top-selling teenage series starring identical twins Jessica and Elizabeth Wakefield and all their friends.

SUPER EDITIONS

> The Class Trip
> The Unicorns Go Hawaiian

SUPERCHILLERS

> The Ghost In the Graveyard
> The Carnival Ghost
> Ghost In The Bell Tower

SWEET VALLEY HIGH

The top-selling teenage series starring identical twins Jessica and Elizabeth Wakefield and all their friends at Sweet Valley High. One new title every month!